Matt had returned to Kane's Crossing to reclaim his memory, his sanity.

He wasn't sure what to do about the wife part, though.

He glanced over at Rachel. She was playing with something on her finger. A ring.

An image assaulted him, making his head swim: a flash of strumming guitars, bougainvillea, sultry nights. But then it was gone.

He reached for his iced tea to chase the dryness from his mouth—and stopped cold.

A little girl stood in the doorway, an urchin with features reminiscent of Rachel's. In his mind's eye, Matt saw the girl dancing on the tops of his shoes, giggling and clinging to his forearms.

'Company, Mummy?' the girl asked.

Reeling, Matt shut his eyes.

Matt Shane had come home…

Available in November 2003 from Silhouette Special Edition

Good Husband Material
by Susan Mallery
(Hometown Heartbreakers)

Tall, Dark and Irresistible
by Joan Elliott Pickart
(The Baby Bet: MacAllister's Gifts)

My Secret Wife
by Cathy Gillen Thacker
(The Deveraux Legacy)

An American Princess
by Tracy Sinclair

Lt Kent: Lone Wolf
by Judith Lyons

The Stranger She Married
by Crystal Green
(Kane's Crossing)

The Stranger She Married

CRYSTAL GREEN

SILHOUETTE®
SPECIAL EDITION™

*Silhouette, Silhouette Special Edition and Colophon are
registered trademarks of Harlequin Books S.A., used under licence.*

*First published in Great Britain 2003
Silhouette Books, Eton House, 18-24 Paradise Road,
Richmond, Surrey TW9 1SR*

© Chris Marie Green 2002

ISBN 0 373 24498 3

23-1103

*Printed and bound in Spain
by Litografia Rosés S.A., Barcelona*

CRYSTAL GREEN

lives in San Diego, California, where she is a humanities teacher. When Crystal isn't writing romances, she enjoys reading, wasting precious time on the internet, overanalysing films, risking her life during police ride-alongs, petting her parents' Maltese dogs and fantasising about being a really great cook.

During school breaks, Crystal spends her time becoming re-addicted to her favourite soap operas, and travelling. Her favourite souvenirs include travel journals—the pages reflecting everything from taking tea in London's Leicester Square to backpacking up endless mountain roads leading to the castles of Sintra, Portugal.

She'd love to hear from her readers at: 8895 Towne Centre Drive, Suite 105-178, San Diego, CA 92122-5542, USA.

**Books by Crystal Green in her
KANE'S CROSSING series**

*The Pregnant Bride
His Arch Enemy's Daughter
The Stranger She Married*

To Gary and Joan.
Your love (and wedding ring) is truly inspirational.

Chapter One

The stranger parked his vintage Cadillac near the breeding barn of Green Oaks, causing Rachel Shane to drop the piece of fencing she struggled to repair.

He walked up the paved road that wound past the maze of white fences and emerald grass, past the pond and the exercise track where her most temperamental thoroughbred, Dolly Llama, was being hand-walked by a trainer.

Rachel didn't recognize him. Nothing about his cowboy boots, faded jeans or long-sleeved denim shirt rang familiar. A Stetson even shaded his gaze from her curiosity. His outlaw stroll caught her eye for a moment, popping a bubble of longing in her chest. She hadn't seen a walk so sexy, so confident in ages, not since her prodigal husband had left her over two years ago.

She sighed and once again bent down to the Kentucky bluegrass, lush and fragrant around her English riding boots, and gripped the fallen white fencing. With a great heave-ho, she hefted the load, then groaned even more loudly than her city-girl muscles did. Overcome with the heaviness of her burden, she dropped the wood, feeling tears of frustration welling in her throat.

What was she doing? She needed to be in the house, watching her daughter, going over the books to see how much money they didn't have to run Green Oaks—this horse-breeding farm.

A trickle of sweat wiggled down the back of her neck, past her braid and into the shirt collar. It felt like a clammy finger, tracing down her spine, warning her.

Again, curiosity plagued her. She peered over a shoulder, more out of habit than anything else. You always had to be watching your back in Kane's Crossing. Too many whispered words could sneak up on you, attacking, wounding.

A voice, its tone reminiscent of low night fires, broke the June morning. "You're going to hurt yourself."

Right. As if Rachel was a stranger to hurt and pain.

This guy was probably looking for a job. As she turned around to see the voice's owner, her mouth parted in preparation to tell him that she couldn't afford to hire anyone right now.

Recognition slammed against her, stealing words, oxygen.

Rachel took a step back. "Matthew?"

He offered a dark half smile, familiar yet unfamiliar all at the same time. A sense of relief seemed to relax his shoulders. "Yeah."

The breath left her body, robbing her of the ability to think clearly. Her pulse raced, the adrenaline a cold shot of reality as it filtered through her veins.

She couldn't say a word, could only stare at the stranger in front of her. A burst of sunshine surrounded his hat, which, in turn, blocked his gaze. But that hardly mattered since she already knew everything about those eyes—how his light brown irises resembled whiskey fumes and the morning-after haziness of a black-tie soirée. She knew that the Stetson was also hiding dark brown hair with a stubborn cowlick, the hallmark of his boyish, carefree charm.

She wanted her first words to her husband to be loving, with all the comfort of a welcome-home embrace. Taking a deep breath, she said, "Where the hell have you been for the past two years?"

Matthew sauntered over to the fencing, leaned against it and tipped up the hat. Finally she could see more of his moody features.

"You're angry with me."

"Angry? I haven't heard from you for what feels like an eternity, Matthew. You haven't bothered to call, and you never even told me you were leaving. What did you do? Confront a midlife crisis? Drive a few hot little red Corvettes around New Orleans?'' She gasped for air, all the rage, all the tear-her-hair-out wondering coming to the surface. ''I hired a private detective to find you and that two hundred thousand dollars you made off with. Chloe Lister found you in Texas after your trail disappeared in the Big Easy, you know.''

Easy. Life had hardly been easy since he'd left.

She snapped out a laugh at the irony, then continued. ''And you haven't answered me, you jerk. Where have you been? And what gives you the guts to come back to Kane's Crossing?''

He peered at his boots, seemingly lost in thought. That's when she realized something.

Matthew had always possessed a canary-eating, know-it-all grin, and, at times, it had driven her nuts. It had been a reflection of his penchant for late-night, Scotch-on-the-rocks schmoozing, his awareness that he could reduce Rachel to a love-starved idiot with a glance.

But that grin had been warped into the now-present half smile, sadness framing it, almost drawing it down.

He looked up, his gaze scanning the paddock, the slash of his dark brows emphasizing crinkles at the corners of his eyes. Crinkles that reminded Rachel of forgotten smiles, of good times past.

"Rachel." He said her name slowly, as if it had somehow found its way inside him and gotten lost.

She waited, wondering if he would wink at her, letting her know that he'd just been out for the last couple of years having the time of his life. That this was all a joke on her.

"It sounds like you've never uttered my name before," she said.

When he turned his attention back to her, she couldn't shake the feeling that it had all the interest of a person you'd meet on a New York subway. Fleeting, short-term.

She pushed a long strand of hair away from her face. "Listen. I've got a lot of work to do. Not that I haven't been able to handle things while you decided to party around the world."

His tall body swayed toward her as he leaned his weight on one jeans-clad leg. "I'm sorry about everything turning out the way it did, Rachel. You'll never know just how sorry."

"Don't you do your apology act on me." Boy, she sounded bitter. Her best friend, Meg Cassidy, had told her, time and again, to think positively. But that was pretty easy for Meg to say, since she had the love of a good man and two beautiful children.

Matthew bent down and picked up the wood with which she'd been battling, handling the fencing like it was so much fluff. Under his shirt, she could see the muscles bulging, labor lean and hard.

As he worked, a sense of belated shock gripped all

the questions she wanted to ask. And she felt thankful for the opportunity to gather her emotions. Matthew was here, *right here*. She'd imagined this scene count- less times while staring at the green-shrouded prop- erty, or lounging in her wide, empty-cool bed. She'd hoped for a reunion in which Matthew threw himself at her feet, acknowledging all the pain he'd slapped into her heart with his absence.

She wanted to hate him. Needed to hate him for all the wrong he'd done her.

It was a while before he had the fencing where he wanted it, accomplishing a feat that would've taken her triple the time. Wherever he'd been, he'd kept busy. That was for sure.

Sweat stains had darkened his shirt, molding the denim to his skin, allowing it to curve over his mus- cles. As Rachel watched his strong hands, she thought of how he used to play her body with the tenderness and slow-bass caress of a Patsy Cline song. How he'd made her heart sing with the melancholy vibrato of a ballad.

Dear Lord, she'd missed her husband.

It was taking all of her willpower to stay clear, to stand back, to see if he'd returned to their horse farm in order to make things right.

Of course, their marriage hadn't been healthy since their honeymoon, a time when they'd loved each other without question or doubt. But that didn't mean Matthew hadn't reconsidered during this recent ab- sence.

Was he here to repair their marriage? He finished his task with the efficiency of a hired hand, then watched her expectantly. "Have I proven my good intentions to you?"

She shook her head. "No. And you haven't done two hundred thousand dollars' worth of work, either."

"Are you always this hard to win over?"

The question struck her as odd. "What, do you think I've changed while you were gone?"

He shrugged, the denim puckering over his broad shoulders. "Maybe you'd like to fill me in on your life, Rachel."

"Why would you care?" She wished her voice hadn't come out like a whip's lash, sharp and cutting.

Matthew's brow darkened, and he tipped his hat. "Maybe this was a big mistake."

He started to walk away and, as he neared Rachel, her skin cried out for him. It tingled with the remembered strokes of his fingers; it flushed with the need for a touch of reassurance.

"Matthew, wait." She turned around. "This is so uncomfortable. So surreal."

Their property glowed around him, gentle hills and rippling ponds, white-slatted buildings and forever-blue sky. He looked as if he didn't belong: hands propped on lean, jeaned hips, worked-over cowboy boot leather eaten by the bluegrass, battered Stetson an eyesore against the pristine Kentucky landscape. If he truly was a part of this business he'd be wearing the typical uniform of jodhpurs tucked into English riding boots, a thoroughbred-set attitude.

But in between their last prime-rib meal together and this moment, he'd turned into a cowboy, and it suited him, bringing out his masculinity.

Rachel wondered if his current age—thirty-three—was too young for Matthew's midlife crisis. She said, "If I tell you my story, will you tell me yours? No bull about it?"

That sexy half smile reappeared on his face.

"Yeah. There's a lot I want to know," he said.

"Well, there's been a lot that happened while you were gone."

Matthew took a step closer. Close enough so Rachel could smell saddle leather and soap.

"I need to know a little more than that, Rachel."

She shook her head, not understanding.

He continued. "I need to know everything because, somewhere along the line, I lost myself."

Rachel glanced sidelong at him. "What are you talking about?"

His smile was not only lacking in confidence, it was downright sheepish. "Amnesia. You're looking at a walking case of the forget-me's."

Oh, this took the cake. "Right, Matthew. Tell me another one."

His face never changed expression. He simply watched her with the patience of a cowboy leaning on his saddle horn and waiting out a sunset.

While fighting to remain calm, Rachel wondered if,

somewhere in his travels, Matthew had improved on his poker face.

Because, right now, she could've sworn that he was telling the truth.

He was lost, all right.

After firing off a barrage of useless questions by the paddock, Rachel had finally led him to their house. At least, he thought it was theirs. More importantly, he wondered if, after the blank wasteland of his missing life, he still held claim to his home, his wife.

Losing your memory, and your life, was something he wouldn't wish on his worst enemy—if he knew who his enemies were.

He'd spent these past two years not knowing he had a family, not realizing that he actually belonged someplace on this big, empty globe of a world. One month ago, Matt had found out that a woman named Rachel Shane was looking for him, had sent out a private investigator to track him down, no less.

The hell of it was, it didn't seem like Rachel Shane wanted him back. Not with the way she'd inspected him like a stud and just as summarily prodded him with her accusations. Matt didn't know this woman from Eve, so he couldn't help feeling a bit torqued.

He watched her as she walked up the path to the shingle-and-stone home. Her slim body, encased by beige jodhpurs and a sun-withered white shirt, had the libidinous appeal of a *Sports Illustrated* swimsuit model, sleek-of-limb and activity-toned. Even if his brain didn't recognize her, his body sure did.

She was making him ache with need, heating him with an odd longing.

Rachel peeked over her shoulder, catching his perusal. A smoky yearning passed over her gray-green eyes, but she tried to cover it by looking away.

Well, baby, he thought, you're not the only one suffering from the hots.

He wondered what it'd been like to feel her skin brush against his, to feel her body pressed against him. Wondered why she hadn't smothered him with kisses when he first walked up that driveway today.

Rachel broke his concentration. "I feel strange, inviting my own husband into our home like this."

Or someone who used to be her husband. Matt wondered what the old Matthew had been like, preamnesia. "Right. This isn't exactly *Leave It to Beaver* domestic bliss."

Though it was damned close. He took in her home's white columns, the bay window, the stone chimney waiting for a good winter smoke. The Colonial serenity seemed foreign to him, surrounded by shrubbery, tickled by trees.

They stopped in front of the door. Rachel said, "I'm going to give you the third degree, Matthew, so you might as well cool down ahead of time with some iced tea."

Matt was pretty sure she didn't even need the ice

to serve it. All this woman had to do was touch the damned glass. "Sounds fine."

She opened the door. "I know, I know. We should've come in through the mudroom. If you've told me once…" Her voice faded.

"I don't remember enough about this place to scold you."

She stopped, sighed. "I have no idea what you remember, Matthew."

He craned his neck, eager to catch a glimpse of his old home, of the place he was determined to reclaim. After discovering his identity and doing some detective work on his own, he'd traveled like lightning back to Kane's Crossing. Back to a life he knew he had to confront.

Not that he was enjoying it one bit.

He took a gander at the furnishings. Gilded mirrors, ferns and shades of celadon met his curiosity. Nothing struck a chord. "We'll talk. Work some things out."

"Sure." She shot him one last glance and started walking again.

They moved through the foyer. Matt noted the soft colors, tasteful rugs, polished antiques. How could he have lived in such a place? He was used to a bunkhouse, decorated by necessity with a bed, rough linens and a hardy night table. That's all he'd needed, until his ranch foreman had told him about the private detective who'd come looking for a certain Matthew Shane. A P.I. who'd tracked him by using a casual statement he'd made to his employer in a New Orleans restaurant. "I'm quitting," he'd said. "Going to Texas so I can lay my hands on what I know. Horses."

Rachel ushered him into a room redolent with the smell of cedar, blackberry and sage. "I'll get that drink."

Her tone was laced with meaning, something he didn't understand. When he nodded in agreement, she seemed half-relieved.

She left him to explore his former abode, making him feel like a traveler who'd just wandered into Frankenstein's castle. Hell, might as well look around to see if anything kicked a memory into gear.

The bay window overlooked elm trees and the paddock with its stables fringing the grass. The ceiling spread upward, shaped like a wide cone, lined with beams. Cast-iron light fixtures lingered on the granite walls, giving the room a slightly monastic flavor. Overstuffed couches choked with heavy pillows capped a limestone floor.

Matt couldn't find the slightest trace of himself anywhere. Not that he knew who the hell he was in the first place.

Frankly, he'd been half hoping to see a reflection of the old Matthew Shane's identity in the books on the shelves, in the turtle shells and crystal goblets set so deliberately on the walnut desk.

Not likely. If this was any indication of the old Matthew, he didn't want anything to do with it. Too poufy for his tastes.

"Have a seat," she said, carrying their beverages in sweating glasses. Ice cubes clinked as he took his glass from her. The hollow sound increased the tension, underlining the emptiness between them.

They sat across the room from each other, each taking tentative sips from their drinks.

Discomfort thickened, breaking through the room's air-conditioned peace. They both started to speak at the same time.

"So— ?"

"Why—?"

Both gestured toward the other. "You go first," they said in stereo.

Matt nodded. "Ladies first."

Rachel smiled, but it didn't convince him that she was any happier.

Her voice confirmed his suspicions. "I'm not sure where to start. Should I tell you where I was born?"

"We've got a lot of time for the fine details. How about the last two years?"

That seemed to put her a little more at ease. Matt only wished he knew why.

She said, "I'd been working some ridiculous hours in the county hospital E.R. as a nurse."

She paused, watching him. Matt shook his head, telling her that he didn't remember.

Rachel continued. "After you left, I—I decided to spend more time at home. I'd always wanted to work with the horses more, and I was happy to volunteer at the Reno Center as their on-call nurse." She flicked a gaze over his blank expression. "The Reno Center is a modern-day orphanage. Does the name Nick Cassidy ring any bells? He came back to Kane's Crossing a couple years ago, played Robin Hood by buying out the town's businesses from the rich people and giving those properties to the poor. Nick started the Reno Center because he was a foster child, too. Remember him from his brief stint at Spencer High School?"

Matt shrugged and tried to grin. This was like listening to a newscast in a foreign country.

"Anyway," she added, "I still work at the center. And I make sure the farm is doing well, keeping the books, doing odd jobs—"

"Why wasn't a hired worker fixing the fencing?" asked Matt. Even if he didn't know Rachel, he didn't enjoy seeing her breaking her back, doing work beyond her physical capacity.

"I can manage." Rachel fluttered her long eyelashes at him while remaining stone-faced.

His body hardened. A lock of hair had escaped from her braid. It was an ash-brown shade, the color of dust from the path of a fallen angel.

Had she been with other men while he'd been lost? The thought pierced through him, a jealous stab.

The skin between his left ribs throbbed, and Matt fisted his hands, hating the reminder. The wound was a slim, pale secret he didn't understand, wouldn't understand unless he could find himself.

Matt said, "I'm not sure you're telling me everything, Rachel. Is this farm solvent?"

Her full lips thinned to a line. "Not after you made off with most of our savings."

Her tone and his damned pulsing scar made him shift on the couch. What kind of man had Matthew Shane been?

"I'm sorry," he said. "I didn't know." He paused. "I've wanted to come back to reclaim what's mine, Rachel. And I'll make up for that money."

"You want the farm?"

She hadn't included herself in the question. That stung his conscience, especially since he wasn't so sure he wanted the family part.

He tried to remain unaffected by her apparent coldness. "Is this a healthy business?"

"In spite of you, we're fine," Rachel took a quick swig from her iced tea, capping the answer. Then, "Am I going to hear your story?"

Damn, his story. What there was of it.

He set down his beverage on a coaster. "It's pretty simple, really. I woke up one morning in New Orleans with the mother of all hangovers. A wino was going through my pockets, but I didn't have anything. No ID, no money. I suppose I'd been mugged. I don't know."

He left out one important detail. The blood on his shirt. Rachel didn't need to know that yet. He'd been covered in the red matter on his left side, evidence of a knife wound that had sliced between his ribs. It'd been superficial, but enough to leave a slight scar.

But then there'd been the blood on the other side.

The side with no wounds. There'd also been coagulated red liquid on his hands, and he couldn't shake the feeling that it was someone else's blood.

It'd kept him from going to the police to find his identity, from going to the hospital. What if he'd committed a crime? Should he have turned himself in?

He'd had no answers, had needed time to think the possibilities through, to listen to the word on the streets.

Rachel gasped at his news. "You don't remember anything?" She paused while he shook his head.

"Damn," she continued. "You obviously don't know that your wallet was found a while ago. It was behind old crates in a New Orleans alley. Some random guy was using your remaining credit cards, so I doubt you were mugged for money."

He couldn't even feel relief at this news. He still had no idea about his past.

Rachel shot another question at him. "Why didn't you get to a hospital?"

"Leave it to a nurse," he said, trying to change the subject. "I only remember commonsense things, no details. Enough to get by in life. I took a job as a dishwasher, but I knew I could do something more. One night, these Texas ranchers came into the restaurant. I cleared the dishes from their table before they ordered after-dinner drinks. When I heard them talking about horses, something sparked inside me. I quit and went to Texas."

Rachel held up a finger. "Well, you didn't go for medical attention then but I still want you to go now, Matthew, to make sure you're okay. Even if you're stubborn as a mule."

At least that hadn't changed about him. "Do you want to hear my story, or not?"

She sat up like an attentive choir girl. "Yes."

"Great." His body tightened as he looked into her eyes. Eyes that reflected a man who'd obviously hurt this woman in the past. The thought didn't sit well with him. "I got a job as a ranch hand near Houston. Menial stuff, mucking out stalls, exercising the stock. Deep down, I knew this wasn't what I was cut out to do. My boss knew it, too, but I was a good worker.

"One day, this feisty gal—a P.I.—came into the foreman's office, asking questions about a Matthew Shane. My boss suspected something, but he didn't give any information. He came to my bunk that night and told me everything she'd said. The private detective left her card, and my boss gave it to me. Told me if I knew anything about this man to call."

Matt didn't add that he himself had done some checking about this Matthew Shane, just to see if he'd been the man who'd done something immoral to coat his hands with someone else's blood. When Matthew's record had turned out clean as a whistle, Matt had decided to return to Kane's Crossing, facing his old life while remaining "Matt Jones," the name he'd given his new identity. Even now, if he dropped the "Jones" part and adapted the last name "Shane," he'd still be the man he'd become in Texas, resuming his former business—horse breeding—and reclaiming his sanity. Bottom line—he'd still be a nobody.

He wasn't sure what he'd do about the wife part, though.

He looked over at her, sitting so primly and properly on the couch. She was playing with something on her finger.

A ring.

An image assaulted him, making his head swim. It was a flash of strumming guitars, bougainvillea, sultry nights spent walking down narrow streets with balconies looming overhead, the scent of saffron floating over seafood.

Then it was gone. Too insignificant to mention. But she must have seen the shock on his face.

"It's my wedding ring," she said, flushing as if she were embarrassed to be caught still wearing it. "Are you okay?"

He reached for his iced tea to chase the dryness from his mouth and nodded.

He stopped cold, his arm stiffening.

A little girl stood in the doorway, an urchin with a searching gaze and pursed lips. Expressions reminiscent of Rachel's.

In his mind's eye he saw the girl swinging through the air with the effort of his arms, her long curly brown hair and eyes—*his* hair and eyes—bouncing and laughing with delight. He saw her dancing on the tops of his shoes, giggling and holding on to his fore-arms for dear life.

"Company, Mommy?" she asked in a voice that couldn't have pulled experience from more than six years of life.

Still reeling with the last image, Matt shut his eyes as the next one assaulted him: a platinum-blond woman and a little boy, posing for a camera, spring-time smiles on their faces.

Problem was, the image didn't look anything like Rachel and this girl who couldn't be anyone other than Matthew Shane's daughter. Problem was, he didn't know who the picture people were.

All he knew was that they had to be an important piece in the puzzle of his past.

But who were they? And why had he remembered them right after seeing Rachel's ring and his own daughter?

Matt's heartbeat thudded in his ears, keeping pace with the throb of his scar, as he squeezed his eyes shut.

Once again, he wondered what kind of life he'd led before leaving Rachel.

Chapter Two

Rachel stood and went to her daughter's side, brushing a cookie crumb from the girl's face. "Tamela, I'd like you to meet someone."

The child wrinkled her nose in Matt's direction. He wondered if she remembered anything about him: what he looked like, what it had been like to hug him.

He only wished *he* could remember more.

Rachel took Tamela by the hand, leading the girl to Matthew. "This is your daughter," she said, a catch in her voice.

At least he could hold on to the few images that had entered his mind. He dropped to the stone floor on one knee, bringing himself eye-to-eye with Tamela. He stuck out a hand for a shake. "How's my girl?"

Rachel shot a cold glance at him, maybe warning him that he'd already gotten too familiar. Well, this was his daughter, for Pete's sake. Again, he got the feeling that Rachel wasn't all that comfortable with his return.

Why?

Tamela stepped toward him, ignoring his outstretched hand, widening her eyes. Matt felt like a snake behind the glass of a zoo exhibit.

"Why did you leave, Daddy?"

Oh, damn. Matt didn't know how to explain this. He drew back from her.

Luckily Rachel stepped in, leaning her knee on the floor, right along with Matt. "Daddy's got a story to tell us, honey. Just keep in mind that we've still got a lot to talk about. Okay?"

Matt's body reacted to Rachel's perfume—a night-blooming jasmine bouquet. The scent was elusive, mysterious, yet somehow comforting. The wildness of it took him back to a dark place. A warm place.

Tamela interrupted his thoughts. "The other day Mommy told Mrs. Cassidy that you're a no-good scoundrel."

Rachel cleared her throat. "That was during your quiet time, Tam. Mommy was joking with Mrs. Cassidy. Adults do that sometimes."

Yeah, Matt was absolutely wheezing with laughter inside. "I'll be honest with you, pumpkin."

At this, Tamela smiled, her brown eyes shining.

Matt wondered if he'd always called her by that pet name.

He continued. "I don't remember much about the past two years. But I'm trying to do the right thing, coming back home. I've lost most of my memory."

"Like you lose a shoe? I did that in school last week. Mommy didn't even get mad at me."

Matt wished Mommy wasn't so mad at him for losing something, either. "I guess it's a little like that. And sometimes that shoe will turn up in the strangest places, when you least expect it. Or sometimes you'll find clues as to where that shoe is. Just like my memory."

"So we can help you find clues?" asked Tamela. She scooted closer to Matt, placing a pudgy hand on his shoulder with all the openness of a child.

Matt's heart choked. He couldn't help the swell of emotion clogging his speech. He wanted to scoop her into his arms, hug her with all the love she'd been missing from him these past two years. Buying time to recover, he glanced at Rachel, whose brows were knitted. Her eyes resembled a mist-covered lake, unmapable.

"Tam," she said, her voice creaky enough to make Matt think she'd been affected, "sometimes memories never come back, and we have to be prepared for that."

Matt wondered if she'd prefer to keep Matthew Shane on the "Missing" side of a milk carton. What would they do if he never remembered his life? Did he have the right to be here, expecting to reclaim his horse farm, his lifestyle?

The little girl nodded stoically, like a minireporter gathering information for *The Toadstool Times.* "Why are you dressed like a country singer?"

Rachel hid a sudden laugh behind her hand, turning away from him. When she recovered, their gazes caught, and he felt fire in his belly—fast-moving and furious. He could almost feel her hair silking down his skin, her breasts sliding over his chest.

Damn, his libido was moving way too quickly. He wasn't even sure he liked Rachel, but something deep inside told him it didn't matter. He felt chemistry between them—a brew that could allow them to make love like strangers, making the tangled sheets hot and sweaty, making the morning-after parting of ways a simple act.

The thought was all too easy, causing Matt to wonder if Matthew Shane had spent much time in roadside bars, roadside motels.

He cleared his throat and answered Tamela's blunt question. "A country singer, huh? Well, I lived in Texas for a while. It's comfortable to wear jeans and a hat when you work on a ranch with horses."

"Like our horses?" she asked, a single dimple lighting one side of her mouth.

"Not really. Down there we have quarter horses, and we use Western saddles, just for a start."

Tamela nodded as if she knew exactly what he was talking about. Matt realized that she'd been raised on this farm, learned to ride with English saddles, on thoroughbreds and saddlebreds.

The whole scene was a lifetime away from Texas flatlands and dust, bluebonnets and horizon-filled sunsets.

The phone rang, and Rachel stood. ''Excuse me.''

As she walked away, she tossed a glance over her shoulder, seemingly worried that he'd revert back to the old Matthew at any moment.

But would that be such a bad thing?

He and Tamela turned to each other, questions drawing them together like time-sharpened hooks.

Rachel walked into the adjoining kitchen, dodging the island cutting block with its hanging cast-iron pots and pans in order to get to the phone. Her heart was still pounding from the sight of Tamela and Matthew, huddled together in the family room. She didn't know why she felt so threatened.

Heck, yes she did. She was afraid the old Matthew had come back to her, bad habits and all. She didn't want to say it was a relief that this new man—this stranger—didn't remember everything Matthew had done to let her and Tamela down, but… Okay, maybe it was a relief.

''Hello?'' she asked, after getting the phone.

''Ms. Shane?'' drawled a crisp, to-the-point voice.

''Chloe Lister?'' Thank goodness. Talk about saved by the bell, or the ringer or…whatever. ''There's no one else in this world I'd rather be talking to right now.''

A deep sigh from the other end of the line. ''Don't tell me. Matthew got there before I could. Dammit, I knew I'd blown it.''

''Listen, Chloe, don't be so hard on yourself. I hired you to find my husband, and obviously you flushed him out. He walked right up to me today while I was working on the farm, just as calm as you please. Like he'd been away on an extended business trip.''

''I understand, Ms. Shane.''

Rachel could imagine Chloe, dressed in a crisp business pants suit with her straight hair cut in a sharp line to the jaw. Vigilant and purposeful, that's why Sam Reno, the county sheriff and a good friend, had recommended Chloe's investigative services.

The woman said, ''I should've known that Texas foreman was lying through his teeth to me. He kept looking at the door, as if expecting the truth to walk in at any time. The man must've gone to Matthew right after I left.''

''You did well, Chloe,'' Rachel said, wandering to the kitchen entrance to spy on Matthew and Tamela. The pair was seated on the couch, laughing together about something or another. A bolt of…what was it— jealousy?…coursed through Rachel at the sight.

Tamela would've been too young to remember Matthew's frequent business trips and the countless parties he'd attended with the thoroughbred set, parties he'd enjoyed without Rachel. She'd opted to stay home with her daughter.

Not that Matthew had been a bad father. He'd showered Tamela with affection, making the child glow whenever he walked into the room. Rachel had to admit that she felt a prod of envy, thinking about how his effortless love won over their daughter every time, while she'd had to take the everyday ups and downs of it.

But hadn't she been living with this protective silence her whole life? She'd done it when she'd seen her mother's sins, kept quiet in order to make sure the family was happy.

She'd lived most of her life in her parents' upstate New York home, dressing like the perfect daughter, smiling at the dinner table as her mother and father asked about her day at prep school. Then she'd hide in her room at night, locking away her mother's secrets with her. Even after Rachel had gone to college, she'd kept her silence. Maybe that was Rachel's destiny—to be the sentinel of domestic happiness, securing all the bad news from those she loved the most.

Rachel shook herself back to the moment as Chloe rounded up the phone call. "I'll be there as soon as I can, Ms. Shane. Expect me tonight."

"Thank you. I'll have dinner waiting, all right?"

Chloe signed off, every bit the professional. Rachel could almost imagine her buffing her shoes and delinting her ensemble before checking in tonight.

She turned off the phone and leaned against the door frame, watching Matthew. She hated to admit it, but he was still capable of seducing her with a glance. Whether he meant to or not.

Maybe it was his light brown eyes, the way they invited a girl to a guaranteed good time. Or maybe it was that half smile, the one that used to smack of arrogance. Now the added melancholy drew her, made her want to smooth a palm over his brow to promise him everything was going to be all right.

Sure. Make those vows you can never keep, Rachel.

Where Matthew used to be light and charming, this man was dark and reticent. Even the achingly uncertain glances he'd slid in her direction were working the old magic on her.

And that body. Matthew had always shadowed her with his height, but he'd gone soft around the edges with his playboy ways, the whiskey-chub around the belt line, the desk-jockey arms. This new guy was all muscle. All temptation.

Don't go back to the way things were, she told herself. Don't fall into his arms for no reason. Don't let that overwhelming sexual draw make you forget that your marriage had become a tattered thing after your extended honeymoon period.

Rachel straightened her spine, donning her protective facade once again. Then she dialed Matthew's family to tell them that their brother had finally come home.

* * *

Matt watched Rachel pace the kitchen floor, phone to her ear, her body flashing past the door every few moments.

He couldn't help himself. He wanted her to look at him again, maybe even smile at him for once. He wanted to know exactly what was going through her mind. Was she calling the men in the white coats to haul him out of her life? Or was she yearning to touch him as much as he wanted to touch her, just to get a taste of what Matthew Shane had once possessed?

Who knows? Maybe touching her would bring back a memory or two. Maybe it'd even make some new ones. Good ones that wouldn't haunt her eyes or make her keep a safe distance.

The knife wound between his ribs pulsed again, reminding him of just how right Rachel was to distrust him. After all, Matthew Shane, the man with blood on his hands, could be his wife's worst nightmare. And did he really want to make her confront that?

Tamela poked him in the arm. "Hey."

"Hey." He shook off the dark mood and focused on the angel next to him. Maybe Matthew hadn't been too bad if he helped create something as wonderful as this child.

"Are you going to tell Mommy to let us stay here? Grandma and Grandpa want us to come back to New York."

Matt tried to keep his cool. "She wants to leave Kane's Crossing?"

"I love it here." She spun a finger through a long, brown curl. Maybe it was a habit. "I love my horse, Booberry, and I love the Cutter's Lake carousel and I love...everything!"

Matt flicked a spiral of hair from her shoulder. It felt like the thing to do. Natural. Expected. "Now why would you and your mommy leave all that?"

Tamela sighed, sounding much older than her years. How much stress had his absence put on his daughter?

"Every time she talks to them on the phone, Mommy cries. Then Mr. Tarkin calls, and she cries even harder."

Tarkin. The name sounded familiar for some reason. Matt thought of ice, ambition, money. "Help your pop out, Tam. Can you tell me about Mr. Tarkin?"

Tamela stuck out her lips and narrowed her eyes, then said, "He's a mean old man, and when he comes to the farm, the trainer and the grooms and everyone else don't smile. He killed Suzy Q."

A horse. Suzy Q. How could Matt remember this piece of trivia when he couldn't remember his own damned life?

"So Mr. Tarkin had Suzy Q put down?" Too late, he wondered if Tamela knew what he meant.

Sharp as a tack, she did. "I heard Mommy on the phone, saying Mr. Tarkin wanted money. That's when Mommy cries the most. When people talk about money."

Matt would have to ask Rachel about Tarkin. If he wanted to go back to his old life, he'd have to know everything about the farm and how it was running.

He felt someone hovering over him. When he looked up, Rachel was standing in back of the couch, seeming none too amused.

"Tam, honey, you want to go upstairs and pick out a nice outfit? Uncle Rick and Aunt Lacey are coming over tonight."

Tamela bounced off the couch and out of the room. Her footsteps pounded up the stairway, leaving Rachel and Matt in a staring contest.

She blinked first. "That was cute. Squeezing information out of a six-year-old."

"It's a hell of a lot easier than talking to you."

"Great. You're back for an hour, and you're already feeling entitled. Glad to see that, Matthew."

Matt stood. "I would've liked the chance to talk with you privately before the relatives hit the scene."

Rachel came out from behind the couch, lifting her chin to look directly into his eyes. The gesture turned him on like a power switch, electrifying him with her spirit.

Damn that chemistry.

She said, "I thought they might want to know that their wayward brother had returned to Kane's Crossing."

He glanced away. "I don't recall siblings."

Silence, unbroken except for the ticking of a clock

somewhere in the room. Hell, it could've even been his time bomb of a conscience.

"I'm sorry," she murmured. "Listen, I'm going to be doing a lot of messing up here, so cut me a little slack."

"Likewise. I can't seem to do anything right."

"That's not…" *Your fault.*

The rest of her sentence went unspoken. Probably because his amnesia very well could've been his fault. And maybe Matthew Shane had brought trouble to the house more than once.

Would she even be surprised if she knew about the blood on his shirt, on his hands? Or had Matthew shed enough proverbial blood on his wife?

The air conditioner kicked on. She was so near, he could smell the jasmine, could feel a stray hair from her braid as it blew past his neck. It tickled him, making him shift his stance.

"I suppose I owe you an explanation about the farm," she said.

He didn't answer, and she didn't pursue the subject. Instead, a heat-heavy silence pulsed around them, pulling them together while wedging them apart.

Dammit, he couldn't stand the small talk, the distance between them. Without thinking of the consequences, Matt reached out and cupped her face between his palms. He caught a glimpse of her stun-parted lips, her wide eyes and flushed skin, before crushing his mouth to hers.

Soft as a gasp, her lips parted beneath his, melting

into the welcome-home greeting he'd been hungering for.

Damn, her skin was so smooth against his calluses, her scent so inviting. In the back of his mind, Matt knew that he'd missed her touch, the long hair that was even now fluttering against his throat.

She pressed against him, nudging his lips with hers. Matt's body reacted instantly, stiffening. He moved his fingers down her face, her jaw, her throat. Her jasmine-mirage perfume teased his senses, filled his mouth with the warm tingle of comfort. Almost like a fine bourbon.

Suddenly, Rachel pulled back from him, as if realizing she was supposed to be angry with the old Matthew.

Every inch of skin above her neckline was as red as rage. "Damn you, Matthew," she said, punctuating the curse by pressing her fingers over her lips.

Maybe she wanted to stop the throbbing, the pulsing he was feeling, too.

"That was more of a homecoming than I got earlier." He tried to keep a straight face, but the very recent memory of the kiss pushed a grin across his mouth.

She lowered her hand, pointing a finger in his direction. "You think this is funny, don't you? You find it amusing that I've had to endure all of this town's gossip, that I've had to walk down the streets of Kane's Crossing acting like I still had some damned pride? Do you realize that every time I'd walk into the Mercantile, Darla's Beauty Shop or even Meg Cassidy's bakery that someone would smirk or snicker or mutter something outright rude to me?''

She overimitated a Kane's Crossing drawl. '''So, Rachel, ya must've driven Matthew away with a cattle prod.' Or, 'Say, Rachel, it takes a lot to scare away a Kane's Crossing boy.'''

Here she took a deep breath, and Matt's heart clenched when he realized that she was on the edge of tears.

But she continued. '''You have no idea what it's been like without you, Matthew. And your coming home hasn't made things much better so far.''

Her words stung, but he deserved it. For being cheeky, for being two years late for dinner, for being her husband.

"I'm sorry, Rachel. I'll say it a million times if I need to.''

A sharp laugh was her prelude to an answer. "Then start now. But a million apologies won't even begin to cover the damage you've done to your daughter.''

Part of him wanted to remind her that he—this man he was right now—had no idea what he'd done to wrong his wife and child. Yet he had the feeling she already knew that. So he decided to stand there, to take the brunt of her pain, to suffer for the other Matthew's sins. There was no other way around it.

She watched him, arms akimbo, eyes flashing. Her chest heaved with the aftermath of her tirade, and her lips were still red and swollen from his kiss.

Damn, he wanted her.

But he backed away to a safe distance, creating a polite buffer. "You might want to take a seat while I complete those I'm-sorries. It could take years."

She exhaled, her shoulders relaxing as she flung up her arms. "I don't know what to do with you."

He was definitely full of suggestions, but he chose to keep them at bay. Instead, he sat on the couch.

Rachel followed him, honoring that physical safety zone between their bodies. She sighed, then softly said, "What makes me angrier than anything is that I need your help."

Matt almost fell off the couch. Was he about to get a reprieve?

Rachel shook her head, and it took Matt a moment to realize that she wasn't answering his silent question, but that she was going to tell him the reason she needed him.

Needed him. He grinned just thinking about it. Then he sobered when he realized that he didn't want to be needed. *Couldn't* be needed in his current state of nobodiness.

"Do you remember Peter Tarkin?" she asked.

Matt shrugged, trying to counteract his still-thumping, kiss-aftermath heartbeat. "All I get are feelings, and they're not good ones."

"All right. Trust your instincts, because they just might help." She sighed. "Your father left you this farm in his will, along with the feed business in Louisville. You used to spend a lot of time up there, working. You loved the challenge. In fact, it took more of your attention than Green Oaks did. Anyway, one thing you inherited right along with this farm was Peter Tarkin, your father's partner, a sixty/forty relationship. Tarkin is a real businessman, a bottom-line kind of guy. If a mare is sickly, if she takes away any profit whatsoever, Tarkin goes for the insurance money, has the horse put down."

Anger ripped through Matt. "This man is a partner? Why didn't we buy him out?"

Rachel seemed to brighten a little at the word *we*. Maybe she felt that Matt considered her a partner, too.

"We tried buying him out, but that's when you disappeared with all our savings. I couldn't afford it anymore. Now Tarkin wants the whole farm, and I've been under such financial pressure with the loss of a miscarried foal that I've been thinking about selling. But I'll be damned if I lose to a greedy jerk like Tarkin."

Matt tried to meet Rachel's eyes, to connect like they had during that kiss. But she averted her gaze, biting her lip. Her withdrawal felt like a physical blow.

"That's my girl," he whispered.

He thought she'd shoot right back at him with "I'm not your girl." But she didn't say anything.

As they stayed silent, he could hear her breathing becoming more uneven every moment. His own heartbeat was even speeding up, matching his breaths to hers.

It was an erotic pause, making him think of the quiet of night, his palm sliding over her belly, up her rib cage, cupping a breast.

His gaze fell to her shirt, the gape of it revealing a tanned patch of skin, the swell of her breasts. Her nipples hardened under that shirt, telling Matt that she was aware of his thoughts. She crossed her arms over her chest.

He girded himself for the truth. "What kind of husband was I?"

Rachel's eyes went wide, her mouth opening with the lack of words.

"Mommy?"

Tamela. And she'd called for Rachel, not him.

Rachel backed away. Matt's rib scar began to heat up again, blazing with memories he should've been able to grasp.

"I'll be right there, Tam." Without another glance, Rachel left the room.

Left him with a wilting sense of discomfort, of knowing that he didn't belong here at all.

Chapter Three

Hours later, under the dark canopy of a June night, Rachel was still distracted by the thought of Matthew's kiss.

As she peered out the kitchen window at the covered, candle-lit dining terrace where her dinner guests were seated, her gaze fell directly on him. In order to greet his siblings during dinner, he'd showered and changed into a fresh set of jeans and a plaid shirt. She'd even convinced him to take off the hat. It'd been a battle, but well worth it, she thought, as the breeze ruffled his dark hair, making his cowlick stand at attention.

A flush burned down her body. He looked like a kid, as gosh-golly full of humor as he'd been during college, when they'd first met with all the bang of a starry-eyed first love. She'd been three years younger than he was, a freshman, light-years more naive, thinking he was the moon and sun all wrapped into one.

Even though they'd gotten married shortly after her graduation, Rachel's adoration of him had lasted for years. It'd outlived their honeymoon, outlived her usefulness.

Tamela scampered into the kitchen, carrying an empty water pitcher. "Where'd you go, Mommy?"

Rachel straightened, taking the pitcher and setting it on the counter. She glanced away from the window, away from her husband. "I'm going to serve dessert. Strawberries over ladyfingers."

Rachel waited for the little girl to stop bouncing on her heels before handing her the first dish.

She smiled at her daughter. "Serve the guests before anyone else."

"Is Daddy a guest?"

Zing. Rachel didn't even know the answer to this one. "Um, he's the reason we're celebrating. Sure, he can have the first one."

Tamela lingered, now swiveling back and forth, making her maroon jumper flare at the knees, making Rachel nervous about her daughter dropping the crystal, shattering it all over the floor.

Tamela gave a saucy little whistle for attention.

In spite of her angst, Rachel held back an exasperated grin. "Yes, Tam?"

"How long is Daddy staying?"

"Oh. Well. We haven't discussed that yet." Rachel nodded to the crowd outside. "Time to serve, honey."

"Is he going on another vacation? Will he find his memory this time?" Tamela wrinkled her nose. "What does he think with right now if he doesn't have all of his brain?"

Rachel wondered what her husband had been thinking with when he'd left her for New Orleans, but she didn't mention it. "It's complicated. Not much is understood about amnesia. It's different for different people."

Tamela nodded. "I sure wish he'd find his memory. He used to bring me those stuffed teddy bears. I'd really like some more of those."

As if on cue, private detective Chloe Lister and Lacey Vedae, Matthew's stepsister, entered the kitchen just in time to spare Rachel from Tamela's inquisition.

Lacey took the dish from the young girl. She was a petite woman in her late twenties, all eyes and lips. When folks around Kane's Crossing talked about the "strange one" in the Shane family, Lacey's name always tipped their tongues. She had a propensity to change images at whim—much like Madonna and her sense of chameleon-restless style. Everyone attributed Lacey's eccentricities to her time in "that home for disturbed girls." Her life was just one more item on Kane's Crossing's gossip list.

This month, she'd adapted a Laura Ashley exterior, her dress flowered, her neck-length dark hair breezy. "My brothers are absolutely dying for some sweets. We need to feed the creatures."

"It's coming," said Rachel, topping off another batch of strawberries with homemade whipped cream.

Chloe Lister stepped farther into the room. "You need more help, Ms. Shane?"

As Rachel handed another full dish to Lacey, it slipped out of her hands, crashing to the floor. Rachel shook her head, trying to keep her cool. "Great. That's just wonderful."

And suddenly, with that one last irritating straw, it was all too much for Rachel. She bent down to clean the mess, and tears clouded her vision.

"Mommy?"

Rachel didn't move, merely held a hand over her eyes. Two long years of waiting. Two long years of lost hope with no answers, even with the return of the man she'd married.

She'd held up pretty well until now.

Lacey's voice floated over the room. "Tamela, why don't you go ahead and serve the men? Leave us with your mom a moment."

As the girl's footsteps faded away, Rachel felt a hand on her shoulder, comforting, calming. A sob heaved through her, embarrassing her. "I'm so sorry."

"For what?" asked Lacey.

Rachel looked up, seeing her sister-in-law, her

hand wiping away a tear from her cheek. Chloe shut
the door, every inch the calm-blooded career woman.
Rachel wouldn't have been surprised if the detective
could stand her ground beneath the attack of a steam-
ing stampede of rhinos, never batting an eyelash.

Rachel said, "I'm sorry for breaking down like
this. It seems I can handle everyone else's problems,
but when it comes to my own, I'm useless."

Lacey laughed. "Nonsense. I'm just surprised this
minibreakdown didn't happen sooner. See, that's
what you get for thumbing your nose at my offer to
help with money for this farm. Even Meg Cassidy,
your best friend, for heaven's sake, wanted to help."

"It would be humiliating to take your money, Lacey."

"Have it your way, trooper." Lacey rubbed a hand
along Rachel's back. "It can't be easy with this amnesia deal. I almost didn't believe Matthew when he
came out with that whopper."

Chloe spoke up. "You can never tell. Ms. Shane,
if you need me to look into it more, I can. And you
can defer payment for a while—"

"Thank you, but no." Rachel took a deep breath.
A woman couldn't ask for much more than good
friends, and Rachel had a whole stockpile of them
right here in Kane's Crossing. How could she think
of going back to New York, giving up on the farm,
giving up on the people who cared?

Her mother used to take advantage of loved ones'
feelings, choosing to consider herself the center of the

universe instead of extending the same courtesy to others. Rachel would never, ever turn out to be a carbon copy.

Lacey helped her up, to the sink, then turned on the faucet. Rachel splashed some cold water over her eyes, her cheeks. There. A little relief.

Her friend said, ''I hope my rascal of a brother has grown up, has changed into the husband he was always capable of being.''

''Things were fine,'' said Rachel, wishing Lacey wasn't quite so astute. Were their dinner-party appearances so strained, so obviously frayed? How many people had noticed the way they rarely spent weekends together? She tried to pretend her heart wasn't breaking apart at the thought of her shattered marital wishes. Just before Matthew had left, their union had faded like the colors of an old wedding cake decoration.

''Uh-huh, absolutely, things were fine,'' said Lacey. Chloe shifted in the corner, probably wishing she could go outside to do more digging into Matthew's mysteries.

Lacey continued. ''You know that men never change, right, Rachel? They just go on and on until somebody puts the screws to them. Well, maybe somebody did a little body work on Matthew down in New Orleans. Maybe somebody did you a favor.''

Rachel wanted to ask, *But what if this new Matthew changes back into the old one? The one who fell out of love with me?*

But she didn't. She kept her tongue, hoping Lacey was right about the new man. Wishing that *this* Matthew Shane could see how much she'd always wanted to win back his love.

Outside, night creatures buzzed and chirped with the deepening shade of the sky. The evening felt like the tepid breath of a watcher, keeping time over the world.

Matt sat by himself and finished the last of his dessert, hardly tasting the summer fruit. He wanted Rachel out here, not hiding in the kitchen as if she wanted no part of him.

He'd sneaked a few peeks at the window, just to see what was keeping her. Lacey and Chloe had gone inside, probably attacking Rachel with girl talk.

Damn. Why couldn't the only person whom he felt halfway familiar with be here, keeping him anchored, sane? He hadn't even remembered his brother and stepsister, and that had made dinner even more awkward.

Matt cast one last glance at the kitchen, then stood, walking away from the house. After ambling around a few minutes, he reached a cool expanse of grass overlooking the white-fenced pond. The sky was purple, graced with streaks of faint star white.

He didn't realize that someone had been following him until he heard a deep voice break the silence.

"The old man wouldn't believe a word you've said about amnesia."

He turned around to see a tall, dark shape. There was a scraping sound, followed by the flare of a match. Faint light skidded over the face of Matt's brother, Rick, emphasizing the hidden darkness in the younger man's gaze.

Rick noticed Matt's scrutiny. "Cigar?"

"No, thanks." God, shouldn't he feel at ease with his own little brother? Shouldn't there have been memories or some kind of emotional pull to ground him? All Matt knew was that Rick flew planes and generally holed himself up in a cabin just off Lacey's wooded property.

There was nothing else Matt knew about his own flesh and blood.

Rick cocked an eyebrow in the star-palled light. Not for the first time, Matt noticed that his brother's hair was the same deep chocolate shade, though Rick wore it a bit longer, scruffier.

The siblings watched the night together, and Matt was positive that they didn't have a damned thing to say. Rick hadn't uttered more than ten words tonight, hadn't even shown much emotion when he welcomed his big brother home.

And then there was his stepsister, Lacey. After jumping into his arms and hugging him near to death, she'd come right out and told him not to worry, that she wasn't as crazy as Kane's Crossing made her out to be.

But who was worried?

Rick blew a plume of smoke in the air. The scent

of brandy and shaded alley corners overcame Matt, making him think of laced grillwork, neon-lit bar signs shining over midnight streets. New Orleans, the place of his rebirth.

Rick said, "Dad would've questioned you up and down about this amnesia, thought you had some angle."

Was he accusing him of something? Matt turned to him, his dander up. "Let me guess. We don't have a very good relationship, do we?"

A grim smile flickered over his brother's lips. "Not after the way you've treated your family the past couple of years. And I don't give much credence to this tragic amnesia story, either."

Before either of them could fire another verbal shot, the roar of a souped-up engine cut the air, followed by jubilant shouts and horn blasts. Both Matt and Rick turned to the commotion.

A cherry-red Camaro zoomed up their drive. A man dangled out of the passenger-door window, waving a ball cap.

"Mattie!"

Rick asked, "You still have questions about your past, Matt?"

He couldn't tear his eyes away from the approaching spectacle. "What the hell do you think?"

Rick chuckled and started sauntering away. He said, over his shoulder, "You're about to get some answers."

And without even a good-night, Rick left.

Matt started to wonder if he should've just stayed in Texas, training horses under his adopted "Matt Jones" name.

As the sports car squealed to a stop outside his home, three bodies tumbled out.

"Mattie!" they all cried in chorus.

He knew he'd regret this, but he approached the car anyway.

Two burly men, attired in tobacco-stained T-shirts, grimy jeans and tractor-logo ball caps flanked a person whom Matt first thought was a young boy. Upon closer inspection, he saw that the third party was actually a tiny woman dressed in tomboy clothing.

"Yee-haw!" cried the female, as she launched herself on Matt. Whiskey fumes washed over his senses as she wrapped her legs around him, smacking a kiss on his cheek.

The other males hefted some liquor bottles out of the car. One said, "We heard ya come back, Mattie! See, I told ya, Sonny, all them rumors are true."

Without missing a beat, the bigger man—Sonny?—stumbled from the driver's side of the car to Matt.

"Aw, lookie here, Junior. Mattie finally decided to throw away them hoity-toity business scrubs. Is your neck red, partner?" He slapped Matt on the back, almost knocking him over with the weight of the wild girl hanging all over him.

Matt tried to laugh off this ridiculous situation. Surely the old Matthew didn't spend time with these people. "Listen, you all. I'm not sure—"

"Duh, Mattie," said the girl who'd, by now, jumped off of him and grabbed the liquor bottle from Sonny. "It's us. Remember?"

They must have seen the fill-in-the-blank of his gaze.

Laughter echoed through the night. Sonny knocked on Matt's head. "Hello in there? Can you believe this, you all? He's ignoring us!"

Matt's hackles rose. This was a nightmare. Or a joke. Yeah, that's it. Rachel had sicced these clowns on him in payment for over two years of her own personal hell.

"All right, you're the Kane's Crossing welcoming committee." He stopped there, noting the trio's miffed expressions.

The girl hung on his arm. "Come on, Mattie. Now that I'm back from Tennessee, we're here to catch you up on all those drinking days you've lost. Farmer Fred's got a bonfire going tonight. And there's a keg there."

"And college girls," said Junior.

A swift kick from the girl clamped Junior's mouth shut. Both Sonny and she muttered, "Damn, Junior."

Matt was starting to get a really bad feeling about this. "Maybe I need to explain something to you all."

Rachel's voice interrupted him. "Junior, Sonny, Mitzi? I thought we'd come to an agreement about this before."

Matt watched his wife emerge from the house. Watched the way her summer dress flowed around her slim body, clinging to the curves of her waist and breasts. As she patiently waited for Junior and Sonny to remove their caps and lower their heads, something primal and unexplainable shot to life in his soul. Something he'd been missing for years.

Mitzi wasn't having any of this respect stuff. "Aw, come on. If Mattie stays home, you'll make him boring. Just like you."

Matt thought boring sounded like a great idea.

Rachel merely sighed, and Matt caught on to her game. A sheriff's Bronco had stealthily pulled up their driveway, sirens and lights off. As a law enforcement officer stepped on to the pavement, the party crashers tried to hide their liquor.

The towering, football-shouldered sheriff came to stand behind Junior and Sonny. His gaze took in Matt before settling on Rachel. "Evening, Rachel."

"Hi, Sam. Back from your honeymoon, I take it?"

Sam. Sam Reno.

Matt's anger at himself burned. Why did he know this name, this insignificant detail?

Rachel still seemed calm, but she was bunching her dress with a fist. She added, "We seem to have a problem here."

Sam glanced at Matt again, and he could feel himself bristling. Was he—the husband—the reason for Rachel's agitation?

"No, wrong problem," said Rachel. "Remember Matthew?"

Matt kept his gaze on her, feeling Sam's stare,

wondering how close Rachel had gotten to this man in Matthew's absence. Jealousy filtered through him, making him stiff with anger.

Then he locked gazes with Sam, who nodded slowly in his direction. There was a total lack of respect written on his face. In a sense, Matt couldn't blame him. If his life turned out to be half as awful as what he suspected, Rachel had every right to hate him.

The tension abated slightly when Sam addressed Sonny, Junior and Mitzi. "I saw the car weaving down the road. You're all stinking drunk. I can smell you from the nearest dry county."

Mitzi grinned. "We're welcoming home our Mattie."

A bottle crashed to the pavement, and whiskey pooled around Junior's feet. "Why, look at that," he said, worming a finger under his hat to scratch his head.

Sam narrowed his eyes as Sonny slapped Junior upside the head. "Junior Crabbe, Sonny Jenks and Mitzi Antle—"

The tiny girl interrupted. "That's Madcap Mitzi—"

Sam continued without a hitch. "Nobody's driving that hot rod home. Let's take a trip to the office."

Matt could feel the weight of Rachel's stare as Sam herded them into the Bronco. He couldn't bring himself to look at her, couldn't take her disappointment.

He was even disappointed in himself. God, had the old Matthew spent time with friends like this?

Sam glanced at Rachel as he prepared to reenter his vehicle. "Maybe you'd both like to come over to my place in a few days? Everyone will want to see you and Matthew, I'm sure."

Rachel looked at Matt, silently asking if he was up to going.

He nodded, knowing that he'd have to deal with the rest of Kane's Crossing soon anyway. There was no escaping the curiosity.

She smiled at Sam. "We'll be there. Tell Ashlyn and Taggert hello."

"I will. Night, Rachel." Sam's grin disappeared. "Matthew."

From the way Sam looked at him, Matt knew he'd be in for a real test when he met Rachel's friends. Hell, the whole town probably thought he'd gone off and cheated on his wife.

The picture of the blond woman with the little boy plowed into Matt's brain again.

He only wished he could be sure that *he* hadn't cheated.

As the sheriff drove away, leaving the blazing-red Camaro in their driveway, Rachel said, "Let's go inside."

A comment escaped his lips before he could stop it. "The sheriff was awfully interested in your comfort."

"Jeez, Matthew." Rachel suddenly seemed so

tired, her eyes reddened as if from crying, her voice weary. "Sam's a friend. You'd be mortified if you could see how much he loves his wife and son."

Matt couldn't move, didn't want to come in the house after revealing his damned insecurity. "You go on in, Rachel, to the guests."

She stood there for a moment more, but Matt turned away from her. He knew she wanted to talk about Sonny and his friends, but what the hell could he say? He couldn't even apologize for this mistake.

He felt her leave, missed the jasmine in the air, missed the opportunity to say he was sorry once again.

Even if Matt Shane had come home, he was lonelier than ever.

Chapter Four

Ten minutes later, their company had cleared the house. Rachel almost missed the crowd already, feeling just about naked without their sheltering small talk, the excuses to work in the kitchen or kick the party crashers' tails back to the nearest jail cell.

She was just descending the stairs after making sure Lacey had readied Tamela for bed before leaving. Matthew sat on a couch in the family room, his head down.

Rachel walked behind him, peering over his shoulder.

He started, noticing her presence, a guilty cast to his eyes. A scrapbook lay in his palms, opened to shots of holly, Christmas ribbons and discarded gift wrap.

She knew he was sorry for what he'd said about Sam Reno. Sam was a good friend who'd just gotten married to the former Ashlyn Spencer, a woman Sam had considered to be the daughter of his worst enemy, the daughter of the man who'd been responsible for the factory death of Sam's father.

Rachel had supported Sam while he'd come to terms with Ashlyn, while he'd fallen in love with her. In return, she and Matthew were going to need all the support they could get from friends like Sam and Ashlyn.

But for the time being, she could ignore Matthew's discomfort and how it had made him jump to conclusions.

Rachel nodded toward the pictures. "The Christmas book. We record every Yuletide season for Tamela."

His lips tightened, and Rachel couldn't help noticing how lost he seemed. He flipped past another page.

"I wasn't in too many pictures, was I?"

She didn't want to tell him that he'd usually come home late from the office on Christmas Eve, bringing Tamela and Rachel generous presents as an apology for being tardy. He'd usually find some excuse to make himself scarce during the Christmas festivities.

Rachel wasn't sure how much information he could handle in the space of one day.

She used her thumb to rub against her wedding ring, a silver trinket etched with roses. Simple, heart-felt. She wouldn't have traded it for all the expensive gifts in the world. The jewelry represented a time when they'd been silly in love, just after college, during their honeymoon in Seville, Spain.

"You're a little camera-shy," she said, deciding to save the workaholic news for another day, a day when he'd had enough time to acclimate himself to his old life. Right now, he didn't need to know about his corporate duties in the feed business. She only wished she could put off all the breadwinner talk forever.

Truth be told, she was enjoying his concern, his remorse for not spending every available moment with her in the past.

Stop it, she told herself. She didn't want to be happy about his amnesia but, darn it, she was liking this new Matthew more and more with each passing hour.

If only she wasn't so afraid that the old Matthew would take his place, leaving her heartbroken once again.

He carefully shut the scrapbook, frowning. Rachel knew he wanted to talk about who he was, what he meant to her. But she couldn't bring herself to do it. Not yet.

He seemed to be lost in thought, his eyes blank.

Rachel cocked her brow, concerned by his stillness. "Matthew?"

He paused, still daydreaming. Then, out of the blue, he asked, "Were those my drinking pals or did they just have the wrong 'Mattie'?"

That was odd, she thought. It almost seemed as if

someone had been changing his batteries. "Matthew, were you listening to me?"

He crossed his arms over his chest. "Yeah, I was listening. Did you hear *my* question?"

She sighed. "You liked to have fun, Matthew. But those were old friends, high school friends. We'd agreed before you left that you wouldn't see them again. Sonny, Junior and Mitzi know better. They're just obnoxious."

Silence hung in the room, a heavy, thick barrier. His minor staring session had clicked something on in her mind.

Sometimes head injuries resulted in epileptic seizures. Rachel wondered if Matthew had just experienced one.

She spoke before he could. "There's something I need to do, for peace of mind."

He glanced up at her. "What's that?"

Pause. "You never saw a doctor, never went to the hospital. May I..." Jeez, this seemed so forward. "May I look at your head? Just to see if there are scars?"

Not that scars would matter two years after the fact. Heck, a CT scan was what he needed. Still, Rachel wanted to at least appease her curiosity.

His expression remained ambivalent. "You sound so clinical, Nurse Rachel."

"Get used to it," she said, knowing that she was coming off as a woman in polished battle gear, armored with concern about the farm, her family.

When he sighed, then looked forward, she took that as agreement. "Thank you."

Holding her breath, she stepped in front of him, shivering as she realized that his eyes were level with her breasts. Warmth flooded her belly, soaking up the desire, pounding in a rhythm that reminded her of slicked skin and whispered kisses.

But those were yesterday's promises, remnants she'd let fly with the wind after Matthew had left. She had no room for them now. There was too much to put back together, too much to contain.

She waited for him to lower his head, but he paused, running a heated gaze over her breasts, her ribs, her stomach. It was almost as if he'd smoothed his hands beneath her thin dress to explore her skin, every aching inch of it.

Time for a blast of reality. She cleared her throat, waiting for him to bow his head and be a good patient. He did, a wicked half smile making the lava in her belly spread down, up, through every hungry pore of her skin.

All right. This might have been the dumbest idea in creation. In fact, in some circles, this would even be considered the first stumbling step toward seduction.

But her heart knew better. It didn't want to hurt again, didn't want Matthew and his good-time charm to toss her misguided feelings like a plastic Frisbee, catching the wind and never coming back.

Rachel straightened, slid her fingers into his hair

and closed her eyes. So soft, so shampoo fine. The strands felt like feather down, thick and shiny.

She used to love running her fingers through his hair. He used to lean back into her while her hands wandered from his head down to his chest. Lower, steamier.

Matthew shifted, bringing her back to reality, opening her eyes. "Find anything?"

Unfortunately she hadn't. Getting him to a doctor would be a priority tomorrow. "Not yet."

She rubbed his scalp, trying to not allow her professional touch to turn into an invitation.

He groaned, low in his throat, and Rachel stepped back, but not before he slid his hands around the backs of her thighs. Rachel stood still, breathless, as he molded his fingers over her legs, moved them up, up, over her rear, her dress whispering over her skin.

"I..." she said softly. What was he—what was *she*—thinking? Wait, she already knew. If Matthew's sex drive had remained the same, he'd be as revved as a NASCAR engine right about now.

And so was she.

Heaven help her, she couldn't even stand, much less think.

Would it hurt to let him touch her for a minute or two? To let him kiss her? To kiss him back?

It'd felt so good when he'd pressed against her this afternoon. She'd almost forgotten about two years' worth of town-induced mortification, night after night full of loneliness and worry. Rachel had just about been transported back to their honeymoon days, dappled with hours of kissing and stroking each other's bodies. They'd had nowhere more important to be than with each other.

But now, *now,* with Matthew's fingers strumming their way toward her heart, it felt just as right. Dammit, why couldn't she remember that it was wrong?

He moved forward as her hands went slack, fingers laced in his hair as she waited for him to...

His lips nudged into her cleavage, and Rachel gasped, her blood racing heat through her limbs, threatening to make her lose all control of her defenses. She automatically moved her hands to the back of his head, pressing, encouraging him.

"Rachel," he whispered against her thin dress material, dampening it with his warm breath, making her breasts stiffen and ache as he circled his thumbs over her hipbones, her belly.

She could feel tears gather in her throat, burning, tugging her body downward until her mouth met his. Her weight pushed them back into the couch cushions, and she positioned her legs on either side of his—bare inner thighs brushing the outside seam of his jeans-encased legs. She felt his growing need for her, and she wedged against it as her tongue parted his lips.

He tasted like spice and man, a heady mixture for a woman who'd done without either one for two years. The combination brought back memories of endless nights in bed, of exotic trips back when they would hold hands for hours and gaze into each others' eyes until they withered closed from lack of sleep.

Matthew wound a hand through her hair, making her feel wild, carefree. He lazed his tongue into her mouth, moving it in time to the rhythm of her memories.

A Seville honeymoon. Moorish cathedrals, sunlined rivers with floating restaurants. A moon ghosting over tiled fountains and slow Spanish dances.

Then came the empty years.

Rachel winced and pulled away from her husband on the clipped breath of an ended kiss. When she recognized the question in his eyes, in the wondering spread of his arms, she stood, straightening her dress.

Seemingly nonplussed, he leaned back on the couch, one arm spread across the top. "I kinda liked that whole medical examination, Rachel. Can I make another appointment?"

She glanced away. "Don't get too worked up."

He chuckled, without any evidence of amusement. "I've been worked up for over two years."

Was he saying that he hadn't slept with anyone all that time? Of course, she hadn't, either, feeling married the entire wait, but... It was hard to believe with Matthew's libido.

She stood straight again, donning her invisible no-more-tears shield. "I didn't find anything, but I want to take you to the doctor first thing tomorrow. And I'd like to suggest that you be tested for sexually transmitted diseases. Agreed?"

At first he seemed taken aback, his jaw stiffening. "Sleeping around during my memory loss was a bad notion, Rachel. It would've meant more trouble for me."

Right, she thought. And I'm the proud new owner of the Brooklyn Bridge.

He must've sensed her disbelief, because he assumed that familiar nothing-bothers-me carelessness, tapping a booted foot with laconic ease. "Whatever you want, Rachel." Then he grinned, the old charm rushing at her full force.

He said, "I didn't get to tell you how much I respect the job you did on this farm." Pause. "Or how beautiful you look in that dress."

She'd heard his compliments before. They'd always made the heat rise, just as it was doing now, bucking up in the far corners of her closed-off world. If this were the old Matthew, they'd already be tripping their way to bed, embracing, covering each other with more suggestive kisses.

But this wasn't the same man, even if he did do the same things to her body.

She made her voice as remote as possible. "Thank you, Matthew."

"I'm going by Matt."

More proof of the difference. Matthew had never liked the nickname. Too informal for the thoroughbred crowd, too lacking in dignity.

"All right then." She started walking away, getting as far from *Matt* as possible. "Now, for more awkward details. I suppose we can put you up in one of our guest rooms.''

His gaze took another slow sweep over her body, and she tensed, afraid of what he might say.

Then, seeing her reaction, his firm jaw hardened. ''Rachel, we both know better than that. I have a much better idea.''

She steeled herself, not wanting to hear it, not wanting to entertain a suggestion that would surely crush her feelings to dust once again.

Maybe a preemptive strike would do the trick. ''Don't you dare say that you want to stay in my room, in my bed.''

''Not a bad idea, Rachel Shane.'' He grinned again, making her blood sing.

''Not a bad idea at all,'' he continued, his grin disappearing. ''Unfortunately, your ardor might do us more harm than good.''

''*My* ardor?''

Matt recognized Rachel's skittish stance, her wide, frightened eyes. He kind of liked when she got all spirited. ''I was thinking of staying at a motel, just until things get a little more comfortable.''

Rachel blew out a sigh. ''Yeah. That sounds reasonable.''

''Great.''

''Good.'' She turned around, ready to go up the stairs. ''By the way, Tamela wants to say good-night to you.''

He stretched up from the couch, his body still

heated from Rachel's most recent kiss. He wanted to reach out to her, pull her back into his arms so he could bury his nose in her flowing hair, kiss her along the edge of her jawline.

The little bit she'd given him hadn't been enough for his appetite.

As she ascended the stairs, he followed, appreciating the sway of her hips below her summer dress. His hands were still burning from slipping beneath the sheer material, from tracing the sleek muscles of her thighs.

Damn, he thought. It wasn't going to be easy to sleep in a motel bed tonight. He'd be staring at the ceiling, cursing under his breath until dawn.

They reached Tamela's room. It was princess pink, filled with stuffed teddy bears, dolls and lace. The little lady herself stood ready for bed, dressed in a cotton nightgown with yellow elephants printed on the hem. Her curly hair was pulled into a ponytail.

"Daddy," she said, "I had fun tonight."

"Me, too, pumpkin," he said, hating himself for stretching the truth. But he *had* felt good while he was with his daughter. The rest of the night just hadn't been so amusing.

Rachel kneeled at the side of the bed, and Tamela joined her. Matt remained standing, not wanting to interfere with the nightly ritual.

When Rachel glanced at him, she must have noticed his discomfort. She simply nodded and didn't say anything.

As Tamela started her prayers, Matt's heart warmed. These were the women in his life and, by some miracle, he'd been delivered back to them.

But his appreciation was short-lived. The doubts invaded him again, the ones that sneered, "What makes you think you deserve a family?"

And he couldn't agree more.

Matt took a subtle step backward, away from the prayers.

"God Bless Mommy, the horsies, Aunt Lacey, Uncle Rick, Grandma, Grandpa and all those other people in the world," said his daughter. The list sounded automatic, especially when she got to "And please bring Daddy back home."

Silence buzzed over the room, and Rachel rested her forehead against her clasped hands. Then Tamela laughed, smiling over at Matt.

"Daddy *is* home," she said.

Rachel gazed at her daughter, and Matt could see her lower lip trembling as she fought for dignity.

He couldn't watch.

Tamela continued her thank-yous, then ended with "God, thank You for bringing my daddy back to us. And please have Mommy smile more. Amen."

Matt coughed to hide an unexpected laugh. Rachel lifted her chin, wiped at her eyes then shot to her feet. All business.

"Well, Tam, why don't you climb into bed?"

The girl bounced beneath the covers. "Daddy gets to read me a story."

Aw, damn. This was going too far. He'd already hurt Rachel. What if he ended up hurting Tamela also? Maybe getting close to these women wasn't such a good idea, especially before he knew everything about himself.

He said, "I'll bet your mom does a better job of telling a story."

Rachel plucked a book from a shelf, then held it out to him. "Be our guest."

The word *guest* reverberated in the air. He got the hint. He could play Daddy, but he shouldn't expect much more than that for now.

And that was fine with him.

He slid Rachel a mock-threatening glance, took the book then settled into a temporary spot on the bed to read to his daughter.

After Tamela had fallen asleep, Rachel followed Matt down the stairway. She'd been planning to say her farewells at his car, then watch him drive back down the path leading to the main road.

But now she wasn't so sure.

While Matt had read to Tamela, Rachel's chest had started burning, then her throat. The sight of her daughter snuggled against Matt's broad chest, his muscled arm curled around Tamela's slight shoulder, had sent spikes of guilt through Rachel.

A big man holding a little girl. He was her protector.

And Tamela was crazy about him, that much was

apparent. Their daughter had been missing a father for over two years. Who was Rachel to take that away from her?

There was also the fact that, in spite of his short-comings as a devoted husband, the old Matthew had been a caring father to Tamela. Depriving him of the opportunity to be a part of the family again seemed vindictive and cruel.

Still…

Matt had reached the front door, his hand on the knob. Rachel shivered as she remembered how that hand had summoned such heat from her skin today, how that hand had helped her put up the fencing.

She needed that hand.

Matt's sexy half smile made Rachel glance away, at the ground.

He said, "Thanks for letting me read to her. You didn't have to do that."

"Yes, I did. You're very good with Tamela. Always have been."

He reached out, smoothed a strand of hair over her ear. Rachel gasped, grabbing his fingers.

They stared at each other, and Rachel could have sworn that, for a moment, he remembered everything about her. The suspicion disappeared when she let go of his hand, breaking contact with his skin.

He said, "I made you cry in Tamela's room. Or something made you cry."

You've made me cry for the past couple of years.
"It's just that…"

He bent down to catch her eye, then followed her gaze back up again until he stood straight. "What?"

God, should she get all sentimental? "Well, this is so stupid. But you used to read poems to me. A long time ago. When you were reading to Tamela, it just reminded me of those days."

This time *he* looked away. "That's something I'd like to remember."

Her voice came out on a wobble. "I wish you could."

In the space of their hesitation, every day of doubt, of wondering what she'd done wrong, pounded her heart.

"Hey, Rache," he said, opening the door, letting in the evening sounds of summer crickets and restless wind, "I'll get out of here. I've caused you enough grief today."

"No, wait."

She sighed. Dammit, she couldn't believe she was about to do this. "This is what I'm thinking, Matt. Tamela should have a family. Now, I'm not inviting you to move into my bedroom or anything, but...maybe we can try..."

"Are you sure this is a good idea?" That stern expression—the one he'd been wearing when he'd strolled up to her this morning—descended and covered him again, blocking her out.

No, it was a terrible idea. But Rachel would keep her peace, just as she'd done with her own mother's secrets, just as she'd done with her own crumbling marriage. She'd use her silence to buy happiness for Tamela. Her daughter would have a whole family, no matter how Rachel struggled with her husband's return.

She tried to seem cavalier about it. "Sure. You can stay in one of the guest rooms."

"A father before a husband. Is that the concept?" he asked, ice in his voice.

Rachel gathered all the steel she'd invented to protect herself from the past two years of embarrassment and hurt. She wrapped herself in her shield, making sure Matt would never guess how hard this was for her. "That's how it has to be, Matt."

He looked away, then nodded. "I'll get my stuff from the car."

When he left, Rachel told herself that he wasn't moving in permanently. He wasn't here to be a husband, just a father. She told herself that, first thing in the morning, she'd call Chloe Lister and take her up on the offer to do more research into the background of the man who'd become Matt Shane over the past two years.

The man who'd turned her life back upside down in the matter of a day.

Chapter Five

The next morning, after Rachel had talked with Chloe Lister and had taken Matt to the city doctor for a checkup, she caught her husband in the barn, trying to make friends with Dolly Llama.

His voice crooned through the immaculate, spacious building, a place where breeding horses ate and slept. "That's a girl. You can be gentle for me, can't you?"

Rachel didn't say a word as she watched. He was attired in full cowboy regalia—Stetson, boots and all. Rachel actually liked the nontraditional outfit; he looked good in fitted, faded jeans.

Dolly, herself, seemed just as comfortable. The pregnant chestnut thoroughbred was in cross ties, which hooked from the halter to separate walls. Usually, Dolly was a terror, a hot-blooded alpha brood-mare, Rachel's best hope for the financial future of Green Oaks. But today she was serene, her big brown eyes dreamy under Matt's ministrations.

He slid his left hand along Dolly's shiny coat as his right hand ran along her length with a soft brush. Rachel's body heated, remembering how he'd explored her own skin last night.

She cleared her throat. "You got right to work."

Matt glanced at her and grinned, keeping his voice even. "No use waiting around. I told the groom to take a break while I acquainted myself with Dolly here."

"Did that groom tell you that Dolly tried to bite him the other day?"

Matt laughed, soft and low. A bedroom laugh, thought Rachel. One that she would've heard while resting her head on his muscled chest in the dark of night.

He said, "Yeah, he told me. He also said that my girl here 'went bad' around the time I left. Sounded like he was blaming me."

"Welcome back to Kane's Crossing. Get used to it."

He kept his silence. The only sound was the brush gleaming down Dolly's coat.

She wondered if she'd offended him, but half of her didn't even care. "That didn't come out the right way."

"I know."

Dolly's ears had spread apart, a sign of mixed feelings, so Matt lowered his voice even more, calming her with his hands. "She's sensing our agitation."

Rachel smoothed her sweaty palms on her denim jodhpurs, hoping she wouldn't spook Dolly. There'd be hell to pay if they ticked off this horse in particular.

"Then, on to a more pleasant subject?" she asked. "Thanks for humoring me with the doctor's visit today."

Dolly's ears returned to the alert, stand-straight position, and Rachel couldn't help feeling relieved. She didn't visit Dolly much; the horse made her nervous.

Matt finished with the soft brush. Rachel automatically took it from him, retrieving the mane and tail comb so Matt could remove tangles.

"The doctor?" he asked. "What a breeze."

Rachel laughed softly. "Don't be so flippant. Taking those antiepileptic pills will help with your seizures."

"They're not a big deal."

"They could be."

The doctor had confirmed Rachel's suspicions: that Matt was actually dealing with petit mal seizures, a mild form of epilepsy earned from the blow to the head he'd suffered in New Orleans. Rachel just hoped there wouldn't be any additional internal damage.

"Well," said Matt, calm as can be, "I'll be going

back to the city so those doctors can conduct more tests. And I've got a real live nurse at home, too.''

"Count yourself lucky," she said, smiling at him.

When he returned that smile, Rachel's heart beat double time. His light brown eyes shimmered over her, starting with her neck, slipping down to her breasts, her stomach, her legs. Then all the way back up, leaving a near-physical sensation of trailing fingertips and heat.

It reminded Rachel that it was possible to forget all her concerns and just fall into bed with Matt. Possible, but not probable, especially if any of those STD tests came back positive.

As Matt finished combing Dolly's tail, he walked toward Rachel, trailing his hand along the horse's hip. Rachel's gaze lingered on the hand, noting its corded strength, its gentle touch.

Don't even think about it, she reminded herself.

For the sake of distraction, she grasped a hoof pick and exchanged it for the mane and tail comb before he asked.

He looked down at the tool. "We make a pretty good team. As far as a working relationship goes, at least.''

Rachel nodded, swallowing hard. "There is that.''

Matt ambled back to Dolly, running his hand down the inside of her front left leg before picking up her hoof to remove the dirt and debris remaining from Dolly's morning exercise.

He said, "So how're we going to keep Peter Tarkin from buying us out?"

She felt a certain pride that, first, she'd kept Tarkin at bay and, second, Matt was asking her advice. "I'm counting on Dolly and her foal. She's our alpha mare, and I paid a stud fee for a prizewinning stallion's sperm. She's carrying the result, and that foal will have one impressive pedigree. The price we get at our next private yearling sale will make or break us."

"We're that close to failure?"

"Yeah. I haven't been current on insurance, and that's how I've been cutting corners. I don't like taking chances like that." She watched him with Dolly, wondering if even the breeding manager had such an innate knowledge of this horse. "She really likes you."

Matt went on to the next hoof. "Give a woman time. I'll convince her to trust me at some point."

He shot a meaningful glance at her, but averted his eyes before she could respond. Rachel wondered if he believed his own bluster. And how could he, not knowing who he was? Not having any information to back up his apparent confidence?

"You know," she said, "your father loved this farm. He'd be tickled to see you in action right now."

Matt paused, moving on to the opposite side of Dolly, where Rachel couldn't see his expression. "In all the excitement, I realized that I know next to nothing about my parents. Could you…?"

His voice was almost wounded, as if he knew how hard his father had been on his pride.

She said, "Your mom and dad both passed away. Years ago."

"I'm sorry to hear that."

He sounded so plaintive, like a child hiding in a corner, ready to receive punishment. But how could she fault that? He didn't remember his parents and, in effect, didn't even know them.

"Your father thought you were capable of anything, even if he had trust issues. He couldn't really let go of the Louisville feed business, especially when you took it over. And your mom had died in a boating accident years ago. Then your dad remarried. He worked as hard as you did, but he didn't have an outlet like this horse farm. He'd already turned it over to you. When he had a stroke, you stepped in full force, 'SuperBusiness Boy' to the rescue. Then when your dad died from a full-fledged heart attack, he left you in charge of the company." Rachel shuffled her riding boot over the dirt floor. "I thought you were walking in his footsteps, Matt."

He moved to the last hoof. "Well, then my change of direction seems to have been a good thing, huh? What happened to the Louisville business when I left Kane's Crossing?"

"What, do you want it back?" *Please, God, no.*

He shrugged. "To tell the truth, I can't work up much curiosity about a business. It doesn't strike a chord in me. Not like Dolly does."

Thank goodness. "Lacey runs Shane Corporations, but she's not nearly as obsessed as you were."

"Lacey?" Even if she couldn't see his face, she could hear the disbelief.

"She admits she's flighty. You always said she can't keep her mind on something for too long, ever since you were kids and she moved into your household with her mom." She realized that Matt had no recollection of this, and added, "Carrie Vedae was your father's second wife. She lives in Vegas now."

He asked, "How about Lacey's whole…"

"Oh, the home for disturbed young girls?" Rachel laughed. "Don't worry. Lacey's in good shape, but she doesn't like to talk about that time in her life. Just a warning, okay?"

"Okay."

"And while we're talking about warnings, I wouldn't bring up the business to Rick. He never wanted anything to do with it." Rachel paused, thinking of Matt's younger brother, the dark shadow of the family, the one nobody really knew. "He's got his own secrets. You used to tell me how much he'd changed since high school. He went off to the Gulf War, and when he came back, he faded away. Didn't want to talk with anyone, didn't want anything to do with the family business."

Matt said, "I got the feeling from dinner last night that we're not the best of friends."

Funny, thought Rachel. All three of the Shane kids

wouldn't—or couldn't—talk about their pasts. They were just about as dysfunctional as her own family.

Matt stood, then made his way over to Rachel, standing inches from her. She had to lift her chin to meet his gaze. The difference in height thrilled a part of her that wouldn't admit to being weak, to being defeated. The part that liked the thought of snuggling into his protective arms.

Softly he said, "I could do with more advice like that."

She should remember his words, even if he hadn't really said them. *More advice, less judgment.*

An amused lilt colored her tone. "Me, Professor Higgins, you, Eliza Doolittle?"

"Close enough."

She could feel his warm breath parting her hair, hear the rustle of his shirt as he moved closer. Couldn't she just bring herself to lay down her head, right over his heart? Couldn't she just allow him to envelop her between his strong arms?

She swayed a little closer.

One of their Queensland Heeler dogs barked outside the barn, spooking her back a couple of steps. The sharp movement elicited a forceful whinny from Dolly, causing Matt to grab the horse's halter, calming her with strokes and tender words. The animal's eyes had gone wide, her mouth caught in a snarl.

As Matt gentled her, Rachel left the barn.

She was expecting Dolly to save the farm, but the horse had already done her share of rescue work.

She'd saved Rachel from completely letting Matt get to her.

* * *

A couple nights later, after a dinner during which Tamela had entertained her mom and dad with tales from her summer school program, Matt read a bedtime story to her again, noting how Rachel lingered in the bedroom corner, watching him. Gauging him.

He still didn't know how to act around her. Husband, guest, nuisance? Miffed, he'd retreated to his own room, concerned about the way both Shane females were breaking down his defenses.

Now, as he lay in bed, staring at the high-beamed ceiling, he thought about their conversation the other afternoon, thought about the information he'd learned about his family.

Thought about the way he'd hovered over Rachel, the wife who'd peered up at him with a wide, uncertain gaze.

Matt rolled to his side and checked the digital bedside clock—2:34 a.m.

He hadn't slept a damned wink in days, ever since he'd settled into the guest room. His mind—what there was of it—was speeding along like a cargo-free freight train without a destination.

Cursing under his breath, Matt tumbled out of bed and slipped into his discarded pajama bottoms. Evidently, in order to save money for the farm, Rachel turned off the air-conditioning at night, preferring instead to sleep with the windows open.

As a bead of sweat shimmied down his bare chest,

Matt ran a hand through his hair, tousling it. Somehow this Kentucky humidity seemed familiar. More familiar than the roads Rachel had driven to get to the doctor's office the other day.

Dammit. He couldn't sit still anymore. He had to do something, anything, to gain back his memory.

Matt crept out of his room, down the hall, down the stairs to the living room. Crickets chanted, their echo hovering over the slight scent of old wood and damp stone. In the dark, the granite-walled house felt like a castle's dungeon—deserted, dark, haunted.

First, Matt wandered over to a grand piano, situated next to the French doors that opened onto an expansive outside patio. He ran his fingers over the mahogany exterior, over the ivory keys, listening as his inspection created muted notes of a discordant song.

Nothing. No memories of sitting down to play a sonata or even "Chopsticks."

Next, he ambled over to the bookshelf, wondering if it held any favorite novels or ideas. *Les Misérables,* Greek myths, *Madame Bovary*. Again, nothing. These must have been showcase books.

But who'd put them there? He or Rachel?

Out of the corner of his eye, he saw a minibar, stocked with gleaming amber liquors and crystal glasses.

He followed his curiosity.

Rachel's voice reined him in. "Isn't it a little late for happy hour?"

Hell, no hour was happy in this house. He turned around to answer, but stopped cold. She wore a flowing white nightie that came to just above her knees, emphasizing those long, sleek calves. Her hair was pinned up, with a few rebellious strands sneaking out to soften her face. With the benefit of moonlight slanting through the windows, she seemed almost ghost-like. A reminder of something in his past.

But instead of a white gown, Matt was seeing the sheer green-blue of a naughtier nightie. He was feeling the burn of long nails scratching over his back, hearing the moan of a woman writhing beneath him.

He couldn't see her face. God, he couldn't even be sure it was Rachel.

Matt thought about his old drinking buddies, the picture of the platinum-blond woman and the little boy. Were these clues adding up to what the old Matthew had been?

Had he been a cheating husband?

The scar between his ribs began to throb, and Matt shuddered, crossing his arms over his chest to hide the pale slash from Rachel.

He tried to make light of the situation, to bury his misgivings. "Doesn't happy hour last all day?"

Rachel's posture stiffened, making Matt regret his words, especially after she'd been so upset about the Sonny, Junior and Mitzi incident.

His wife swept down the stairs, past him, to the bar. She splashed a shot of bourbon into a glass and held it out to him. "Here you go, Matthew. Party on."

He ignored the gesture. "What the hell are you about, Rachel?"

She didn't put the drink down. "I'm your enabler. Remember? I'm the woman who waits at home and looks after your child while you hobnob with the thoroughbred set. I'm the idiot who doesn't say a damned word when you miss the dinner you promised to eat with your family. I'm the airhead who—"

She cut herself off, folding her arms over her chest, gaze lowered.

"Who what?" he asked. The image he was getting of the old Matthew was growing worse by the minute.

A sharp laugh escaped her. "It's funny, really. My parents thought I'd made such a big mistake when I married you. They thought you'd be a spoiled rich boy, a playboy in the rough."

He almost didn't want to ask. "Were they right?"

Rachel pursed her lips together. Maybe she was fighting the words.

Softly she said, "I never lost hope that you'd turn it around. But then you disappeared and… Well, let's just say I never bought you a T-shirt that read World's Number-One Hubby."

Matt was hating himself more and more. How could he have taken such a beautiful daughter and wife for granted? How could he ever redeem himself?

Hell, the answer was easy. He couldn't redeem himself. That was the problem.

"Listen, Matt," she said. "I'm sorry to take this out on you. It's almost like using a whipping boy."

She put down the bourbon. "I can't believe I shoved that booze in your face. But… I was just wondering if you'd drink it. If there was any of the old guy left in you."

Matt relaxed his stance, but still kept a palm over his scar. He wanted to hold Rachel, to tell her that there was some solution to this big mess. But at the same time, he couldn't bring himself to close the distance.

"Hey," he said. "If it makes you feel any better, I don't really drink. I like a good beer every once in a while, but that's about it."

A slight smile wavered over her mouth. The mouth he'd kissed the other day.

"It wasn't the drinking. It was the fact that Tamela and I never saw enough of you. I used to think you didn't want to come home for some reason, and partying was your excuse to stay away."

Matt wondered if he'd start feeling that way again. If the old Matthew would seep into his bones just because he was home again. Just because he was reborn to be bad.

Rachel cleared her throat, adjusted the slipping neckline of her nightie. "At any rate, talking about this isn't doing any good. I'm still too angry."

"Great."

She shrugged. "I feel like I'm yelling at a puppy who doesn't understand what I mean."

Matt tried to laugh, to make it seem like it didn't matter. "I take your meaning. I've been in the doghouse since I got here."

Rachel laughed, really laughed, at that one. It felt good to coax an emotion that wasn't stilted or just this side of civil.

She said, "At least you've retained your sense of humor."

"It's good to know I had one."

A gust of wind blew the sheer French door curtains off the patio, a spectral flutter on the edges of the room. Rachel's gaze followed the breeze, and she came out from behind the bar, extending a hand.

"Come here for a second," she said.

He followed her, enfolding her fingers in his own. A bolt of recognition, of tenderness, shot through him as he ran a thumb over her soft skin.

And to think of the time he'd wasted touching the objects in this room, hoping for a moment of clarity. All he'd had to do was touch Rachel again.

They walked to the French doors and into the night. The faint scent of horse and grass greeted them as they leaned on the stone railing. The wind toyed with the hem of her nightie, making Matt hope the elements would win this round.

As he watched her, Matt noticed Rachel's perusal of him; her gaze had settled on his bare chest, and he could've sworn that her gray-green eyes had gone misty. He turned away from her, taking care to shield his scar.

"What's out here?" he asked.

Rachel straightened, gesturing to the glow of light beyond Green Oaks. "Main Street, Kane's Crossing. Are you ready to deal with them tomorrow when we go to Sam's house?"

Oh, yeah. Matt had almost blissfully forgotten. "No chance of a rain check?"

"It'll have to happen sooner or later. You're going to meet people who don't hold back in the opinion department, just like me. So be ready."

"I can handle it." Boy, did he sound studly. Now if he could only back it up with fact.

He scanned the landscape, noticing a dark house looming against the sky. It seemed familiar. "Whose home is that?"

Rachel followed his pointing finger. "That's where Nick and Meg Cassidy live. You'll meet them tomorrow. Meg's my best friend. But—here's more advice—don't listen to any of the rumors about their twin son and daughter."

"Why?"

"Oh, yeesh. Here we go with the Kane's Crossing gossip."

"Hey, you're my Henry Higgins, sugar."

She gasped, her eyes welling with tears. He must've called her "sugar" in the past.

After a moment, she answered. "The gossips said that the mighty Chad Spencer, who's cowering in Europe with the rest of his criminal family, fathered

Meg's twins. Nick is their daddy, though. And don't forget that. Got it?''

"Got it." He inched nearer to Rachel, drawn by her jasmine scent. Damn, he wanted her.

She tilted up her chin, her eyes fringed with incredibly long, dark lashes. Matt leaned toward her, and her eyelids fluttered shut, her lips parted slightly.

Closer still. Near enough to feel the heat of her skin. Far enough to know that this wouldn't be a kiss of passion or lust.

If Matt were to kiss his wife now, he'd be committing himself. He'd be investing his heart in something that he wasn't ready—or willing—to accept.

He backed away, folding his arms across his chest—his scar—once again. "Thank you, Rachel," he said.

As he moved through the French doors, he could've sworn he heard a long sigh.

Maybe Rachel was close to welcoming him back home. But Matt wondered if he would ever be ready himself.

Chapter Six

Sam and Ashlyn Reno's all-American clapboard home rang with the sounds of giggling children. As Matt and Rachel pulled up in his Caddy, Rachel pointed out who was whom: there was eight-year-old Taggert Reno running through the spray of a hose in his swimming trunks while his adoptive mother, Ashlyn, aimed the water at him; Sam Reno, dressed in khakis and a T-shirt, standing guard at the grill, lighting the barbecue coals; Sam's foster brother, Nick Cassidy and his wife, Meg, arranging sun hats and smoothing sunscreen over their umbrella-covered, playpen-bound toddler twins; and, of course, old Deacon Chaney, the manager of the Mercantile Department Store and owner of the town's newly opened

Chaney's Drugstore, swatting flies from his face while resting on the porch.

As Matt pulled to a stop, Tamela jumped excitedly up and down in the back seat. She was already stripped down to her bathing suit. "Can I play with Tag?"

"Wait," said Rachel. "Let's get some sunblock on you first."

After Tamela was lotioned up, she sprinted from the car and joined Taggert in his water play.

Rachel placed a hand over Matt's. "Ready?"

He tried not to feel like a man who was about to go on trial. "Sure."

She squeezed his fingers and, after fitting his hat on his head, they left the car.

Following a general welcome from everyone, Meg led Rachel to the kitchen, as Matt grabbed an iced bottle of grape soda from the cooler.

He watched his daughter squealing and running through the water as Ashlyn Reno handed the hose to Taggert and joined the women in the house.

Great, he was deserted now. Stranded with three men who looked like they didn't know how to say boo to each other.

Matt straightened his spine, trying to project an image that said standing in the middle of a barbecue with his hand jammed in his jeans pocket and being stared at was fine with him. From the corner of his gaze, he saw Nick Cassidy nod to Deacon Chaney.

Both of them wandered over, extending their hands in greeting.

Nick hooked his thumbs into his belt loops, his beer bottle dangling between two fingers. "I guess we're the official greeting committee for Kane's Crossing. Isn't that so, Deacon?"

The old man shrugged. "I didn't volunteer for such nonsense."

Sam Reno wandered over to them, brushing ice slivers from a soda can. "Sorry to tell you two, but Sonny, Junior and the recently returned Mitzi Antle beat you to it."

He told them the story, reducing Nick and Deacon to grim smiles.

Nick sipped from his beer, then said, "If Sonny and Junior weren't such inept bullies, I'd be offended for you, Matthew."

Damn that name. "It's Matt now," he said.

The men acknowledged that tidbit with stilted nods. They sipped from their beverages, slapped at some flies.

Finally Matt decided to put an end to their discomfort. "I know. You all are wondering just what happened to me. You're wondering about the amnesia and how I got it in the first place."

Nick and Sam both started to deny it, but Deacon interrupted.

"Hell, yeah, I'm wonderin'. What's a Kane's Crossing boy doing in Louisiana? Things aren't exciting enough here?"

Matt laughed. "I think I could learn to like the pace of things." Then he explained everything he knew: how he'd awakened without an identity, how he'd worked on the ranch, how Chloe had found him.

Nick responded with a low whistle. "Meg would've killed me with that redheaded, sweet-sour temper of hers. But Rachel…"

Sam wasn't smiling. "I can't believe Rachel hasn't strung you up by the thumbs. Even if she didn't show it, she was a wreck while you were gone."

That too-familiar jealousy threatened to explode out of Matt's fists, straight to Sam's jaw. "Listen, Sam, I'm—"

Deacon held up his hands like a referee calling a foul. "Boys. I'd like to enjoy my barbecued hot dogs without indigestion. Let's pack away the hard feelings."

Jeez, he'd been told off. Yet he was somewhat grateful to Deacon for putting an end to the conversation.

But Sam was right. Even now, Rachel must have been scared to death that the old Matthew would resurface any day, that he'd go right back to making her sleep on a pillow wet with tears.

The thought made him feel guiltier than ever. It made him realize that he couldn't fall for Rachel and she couldn't fall for him, because, if he did regain his memory, he'd just return to his old habits, hurting Rachel again. And that was the last thing he wanted, the last thing *she* needed.

Obviously Sam wasn't ready to let the matter drop. "Deacon, are you so damned surprised that he treated Rachel like dirt? This—" he indicated Matt with an opened palm "—is the guy who played demolition derby with all the girls' hearts when we were in high school."

He turned to Matt. "You probably don't remember prom night."

Part of him wished he did, but the other part was relieved. "No, I don't."

An expression of near pity crossed Sam's stern face. "You played four girls against each other. In the gym, while everyone was dressed in rented tuxes and foofy dresses, those girls fought like demons. It ruined everybody's night, especially mine. I was dating one of those girls."

Nick laugh-coughed into a hand, and Deacon grumbled, "That's high school, Sam. I'm hoping you've gotten over it by now."

"What the hell do you think, Deacon?" Sam actually laughed. "I love Ashlyn more than anything on earth, even more than those stupid memories from when I was a kid. But, Matt, that was just an example of the old days. And, I have to say, you didn't change much."

Deacon piped up. "That's the truth. You could've given Hugh Hefner some playboy lessons."

Nick, who'd remained fairly silent until now, spoke up. "Seems to me that Matt's got a shot at starting over."

His pale blue eyes bored straight into Matt's. "You've got a real miracle on your hands, if you don't blow it."

They were all quiet as Nick's words sunk in.

The harmony of female laughs floated over the summer air as Meg, Ashlyn and Rachel stepped out of the house and onto the porch, where they settled into waiting lawn chairs.

When Matt looked at his wife, he found her watching him, her eyes doe-wide, her fingers absently rubbing her soda glass.

What if he left her now? Would he alleviate her stress? Make her life easier by removing the reminder of her old life?

Tamela's giggles filtered through his consciousness. He turned to his daughter, wondering if, at least, *she* was ready to forgive her daddy his sins.

Matt excused himself from the group of men and headed toward Tamela, determined to appreciate her smile, her pure love.

Who knew how much time he had left before he reverted back to his true self?

Rachel was watching her husband zap Taggert and Tamela with spurts of water when Meg Cassidy sighed and said, "What do you guess those men were talking about?"

"What do you think?" answered Ashlyn Reno. She was cradling two cloud-soft Maltese dogs in her lap. Ashlyn and Sam had adopted the pets after her parents had left them behind while escaping the country for their crimes.

Thank goodness they'd already discussed Rachel's business in the kitchen, because she didn't want to let go of the image of Matt laughing with her daughter, of Tamela running to her father and flicking droplets into his face, of him crushing her to his chest in a loving hug.

Last night, when she'd tempted Matt with the bourbon—and herself, she had to admit—he'd refused. On both counts.

Had Matt fallen completely out of love with her? The same heated gaze still lingered over her body with desire burned into his brown eyes. He still touched her the same way, unleashing that sizzling expectation she always had when he was too near.

Sure, he reacted physically to her. He'd always done so.

But did he harbor feelings for her? Feelings he'd lost somewhere down the line?

Rachel shook herself, realizing that Meg and Ashlyn were staring at her. "Whoops," she said.

Ashlyn bit back a smile, casually smoothing pixie-short hair away from her face. "I know what that 'whoops' means."

"I speak that language, too," said Meg, green eyes flashing with humor. "Of course, I became very fluent in 'whoops' around the time Nick and I were falling in love. You, too, Ashlyn?"

"Oh, yeah. I'm still learning the subtleties of 'whoops.' I'm a newlywed. Remember?"

Rachel shook her head. "Speaking of which—"

Meg shrugged. "She's changing the subject—"

"How was the honeymoon, Ashlyn?"

The younger woman's rainbow-colored eyes went dreamy. "Florence was gorgeous. Perfect. And I'll always worship Meg and Nick for taking care of Taggert while we were in Italy."

"The more kids the better." Meg tried to look innocent, puckering her lips in a mock whistle.

"What are you trying to tell us?" asked Rachel.

Meg leaned forward, encouraging Ashlyn and Rachel to follow suit. "Nick and I are having a baby! Can you believe that? I'm two months along."

Rachel's heart fluttered. She was one of the few people in Kane's Crossing who knew that the twins were really Chad Spencer's kids. Nick had claimed them, but Meg and Nick having their own children was certainly an additional blessing.

Tears came to Ashlyn's eyes. "That's beautiful, Meg." She paused. "I wasn't going to say anything today, but this is just too perfect."

Rachel cupped her hands over her mouth. "You, too?"

Ashlyn broke out into a grin. "Yeah. I'm probably a few weeks behind you, Meg! They'll almost be twin cousins!"

The two women embraced each other, crying with happiness.

Rachel rubbed their backs, ecstatic for them, yet oddly distanced.

She shot another glance over to six-year-old Tamela, then over to Matt. Would Rachel ever have another child with him? Was it even a good idea?

After all, the old Matthew hadn't even...

Meg reached out to include Rachel in the group hug. She whispered, "I'm so happy that Matthew's come home. All three of us have added to our families."

Rachel only wished she could feel as secure with her new addition as the other women did.

About an hour later, after the hot dogs and hamburgers had been thrown onto the grill, the good citizens of Kane's Crossing started to arrive.

Meg smoothed a palm over Rachel's back. "I swear, none of us invited these people."

Rachel merely watched as everyone from Mrs. Spindlebund of the ladies' auxiliary to Mayor Strevels made their way up the Renos' driveway carrying cucumber salads, gelatin molds and chocolate-chip cookies.

Rachel said, "News just travels faster and faster in these parts."

"Good old Kane's Crossing," said Meg, rolling her eyes.

She patted Meg on the arm and spied her husband across the lawn. He was shaded by a massive oak tree, his arms crossed, almost daring the townspeople to approach him.

Rachel walked past the picnic table full of children, toward Matt. Might as well give him a little support, nip the town gossip in the bud before they saw them camped on opposite sides of the barbecue.

He relaxed his stance when he saw Rachel approaching. "What's this? Some kind of massive pilgrimage?"

"You know human nature. People in this town are rubberneckers, desperate to find a nasty accident to keep their minds occupied."

She stood beside him, trying to keep her eyes off the muscles bulging beneath his thin, white T-shirt. Even the thought of his tight, rope-bunched arms made Rachel a little breathless. "They look like circling vultures, don't they? I wonder who'll be brave enough to say hi first."

"Don't ask me," he said, a half smile making the crinkles around his light brown eyes deepen. "I'm not a betting man."

"Good thing. You were terrible at poker." She shrugged. "Not that it stopped you from gambling with Sonny and the gang every Friday night."

"Yeah. Sam was kind enough to inform me of a few past antics while we were man talking."

Rachel swallowed away a sudden lump of sadness. She wished she could've been there to protect him. But, then again, she'd done too much protecting as far as Matthew—and her mother—had been concerned. Maybe it was time to stop.

By now, the barbecue was clogged with townsfolk. And they were hovering nearer to Matt and Rachel.

She closed her eyes for a moment, fighting a panic. Once, when she was nine, she'd been playing outside during a family vacation—one of those trips her parents had dragged her on so they could "rebond." It had actually been one of many marriage repair trips, she'd realized once she'd been sent away to college.

But that hadn't mattered when she was a girl. All she knew was that she'd needed to get outside, away from the buzz of her parents' voices as they argued in the rented cottage. She'd wanted to go far away, to block out their harsh words. So she'd backed into a bush. Into a beehive.

Rachel could still feel the stings, the breath-robbing fear of being smothered by angry sounds and pain.

That's how she felt now, waiting for everyone to confront her and her husband.

She linked her arm through his, holding back a shiver of desire at the feel of his humidity-slicked, solid arm.

Matt peered down at her, the shade from his hat not quite covering the stunned blink of an eye. He reached over and laid his hand upon hers.

Mrs. Spindlebund was the first to approach.

Although she was short in stature, she managed to look down her nose at them, her salt-and-pepper hair glittering in the sun. "Well, Matthew Shane. The ladies' auxiliary is happy to see that you survived your vacation.''

If she was fishing for information, she'd get none of it here. Rachel sighed. ''Thank you, Mrs. Spindlebund. Goodbye.''

The elderly woman's mouth flew open in shock.

Rachel held up a finger, silencing any incoming remarks. She hadn't spent two years slapping away Kane's Crossing gossip to lose her dignity at this moment.

''Thank you, Mrs. Spindlebund.''

The woman ''humphed'' and minced away, leaving Matt chuckling.

''That was efficient,'' he said.

''Yeah. She'll probably take her snickerdoodles and stomp out of the barbecue. Watch me cry tears of sorrow.''

Matt made a whistling sound. ''Thank goodness I'm not the object of your barbs now.''

''Can't promise how long that'll last,'' she said, pasting a fake smile on her face as the mayor approached.

Matt's half grin disappeared along with their moment of peace. Rachel knew she'd shut him out once again with her sharp words, but she couldn't think of a better way to protect herself.

At the barbecue, people came, people went. And just when Rachel thought the worst of it was over, Peter Tarkin showed up.

By now, Matt had folded his long body into a lawn

chair, and Rachel had done so, as well. When she caught a glimpse of their horse farm business partner from across the lawn, Rachel gasped.

"I can't believe he showed his face."

"Who?"

"Tarkin. And—oh, my—not to be outdone, he's brought along his fiancée." She groaned. "That poor woman."

Matt was attempting to be casual; she could tell by the way he was sitting back ever so carelessly while he cocked an eyebrow. That was his "tell," the reason she could beat his pants off at poker any day of the week. Whenever he was incredibly concerned, he'd lift that eyebrow.

He asked, "Is he the short man with silver hair on the sides of his face?"

"Yeah. Very Count Dracula, don't you think?"

"Who's the woman?"

Rachel cringed as she glanced at Matt, expecting him to stay true to his reputation and be running an appreciative eye over Tarkin's fiancée. But he merely seemed cautious.

She sighed her relief. "She's Daisy Cox. Used to live in Kane's Crossing, but only sporadically. I guess she used to skip school to go to her beauty pageants. She was Miss Spencer County a while ago."

Matt nodded, then looked back at Rachel. He grinned, as if he knew exactly how she'd been wondering about his libido and how that libido was reacting to beauty-queen women. "*You* could've been Miss America."

"Stop it, Matt."

He lifted his hands, palms up. Surrendering.

Rachel peeked back at Daisy. Blond, with ringlets coursing down her back, Saks Fifth Avenue wardrobe... Yet Daisy wasn't smiling. She walked two steps behind Tarkin, as if she were a trophy being trailed behind an unappreciative owner.

Not surprisingly, the town's ever-attentive grapevine had reported that Daisy had gained some weight after being crowned Miss Spencer County. Sure, she was comfortably padded, thought Rachel. But Daisy was by no means "fat."

And from the way Peter Tarkin was marching through the crowd, ignoring his "loved one," Rachel wondered what kind of marriage this would be.

Tarkin slid up to her and Matt, nodding at her in acknowledgment, bending down to shake Matt's hand.

"Welcome back," he said, his stiff jaw giving the trite phrase more meaning than usual.

Rachel stood, tired of the scrutiny, tired of facing people with a smile that weighed like an old secret. "If you'll excuse us, Mr. Tarkin, we need to be going."

"Of course," he said, analyzing Matt as he rose from his seat to tower over Tarkin.

A few steps away, Daisy shyly smiled at Rachel as she waited behind her fiancé.

Rachel politely grinned back and held out her hand for Matt, and he grabbed it, squeezing her fingers in silent support. They started walking away.

But Tarkin wasn't done talking. "I'll be calling on you soon, Rachel. And don't think it'll be a social call."

Matt whipped around, facing the businessman. "You'd better come prepared."

The older man nodded, a slight tilt to his thin lips. "I'm looking forward to it, Mr. Shane."

Matt slipped her hand into his again, making sure she walked beside him as they left.

Maybe he'd recognized how Tarkin's fiancée walked a few steps behind her intended. Was Matt telling Rachel that they were equal partners? That they could solve their problems together?

God, this new Matt was too good to be true.

But in the meantime, what was Chloe Lister finding out in New Orleans? Would she be uncovering information that would invite the old Matthew to come wandering back into Rachel's life?

And would the old Matthew end up chasing away this new one?

Rachel grabbed on to Matt's hand even tighter, suddenly unwilling to let him go.

Chapter Seven

After a very restless night of longing, Rachel rose early the next morning, intent on scouring the horse farm's account books for creative ways of making their enterprise stronger.

But no matter how hard she tried to concentrate, it was no use.

She kept thinking of the way Matt had supported her yesterday, watching her back when Tarkin had threatened her. She kept thinking of the way Matt had kept his cool while keeping up his guard.

Even after she'd picked up Tamela from summer school, Rachel had given the books another shot. But she might as well have been staring at the wall for all the good it was doing.

She tossed her pencil onto the desk, watching as it landed on the eraser and bounced to the carpet.

Balancing the books was useless, not only because it seemed impossible to run the farm with their present income, but because all her brain cells were occupied by Matt.

A door thumped shut in the rear of the house. She peered at her watch—4:00. Matt would've been working on the farm, returning home to replay their farcical marriage for yet another night. A night in which both of them slept in different beds, different worlds.

She heard him climb the stairs. Heard the water flow through the old pipes as he took a shower. She waited, imagining the water as it glistened over his skin, over every hard curve of muscle. When the shower stopped, Rachel bolted upright in her chair.

"Forget this," she muttered, pushing back from the desk with such force that her chair clumped to the ground.

As she ascended the stairs, thoughts screamed through her head. *We got along so well yesterday. What would be the harm in spending a little time with him?*

What would be the harm?

At the top of the stairway, she took a deep breath, calmed her accelerated heartbeat.

Just knock on his door, she told herself. Ask how his day went. Ask if he'd mind resuming that husband/wife relationship you miss so much....

She stood before his door, hand raised to thump on the wood.

Oh, boy. What was she doing? Matt had just come into the house, and here she was, zipping right over to beg for his attention. Rachel felt like the thirteen-year old dork who had a crush on the prom king.

Nope. She wouldn't knock. Terrible idea. Why reveal her hand—her longings—before he'd even been home two weeks?

"Nerd," she said to herself, backing away from the door so she could return to her own room. Locking herself away from Matt seemed to be the safest course of action.

But before she could move, Matt opened the door.

The first thing she saw was his broad, bare chest. Drops of water squiggled their way down his tanned skin. A few rivulets had been caught by the dusting of dark hair traveling his flat belly to the edge of a fluffy, white towel tucked around his lean hips.

Rachel couldn't swallow. Couldn't talk. She was too pleasantly stunned to communicate with anything but her gaping mouth and saucer-span eyes.

Once upon a time, she'd combed her fingers over that chest.

After giving her plenty of time to speak, Matt leaned against the door frame, his half smile indicating that he could read every naughty thought that was streaking across her mind.

His voice was midnight-hour low. "Afternoon, Rache."

She tried to respond, but all that would come out of her mouth was a tiny mewing sound.

Get yourself together, she thought.

She was much more successful the second time around. "I thought I heard you come upstairs."

Good heavens, that was brilliant. Where had the comeback queen gone? She'd never lacked for anything relevant to say.

He pushed back a hank of dark, wet hair that had slumped over his amber eyes. A gleam of mischief sparkled in his gaze. "Yup, that was me, all right. Can I do something for you?"

His lazy, Texas-tinged drawl—no, his near nakedness—was tempting Rachel to drop her proper facade. She wanted to answer his double-edged question with an innuendo of her own, running both her hands up his chest while guiding him back into his room. To the bed.

Don't do it, warned the side of her that still had a brain. The side that still knew what it meant to feel the two-years-plus worth of suffering and doubt Matthew had caused.

She cleared her throat, clasping her hands in front of her in order to keep them out of trouble. "Any dinner requests for tonight?"

And she'd thought that she couldn't sound any dumber.

Matt opened the door a little wider, as if inviting her in. You know what you're missing, he seemed to be saying.

"Actually," he said, "I was thinking of giving you the night off. Going into Kane's Crossing, grabbing something to eat, seeing a movie."

Dinner, a movie. Rachel hadn't treated herself to such luxuries for some time, thinking that she could cut corners by depriving herself of amusement.

She thought of the accounting books. "I'm not sure, Matt...."

"It doesn't have to be anything fancy. I just thought we could use a change of setting."

She was touched by his thoughtfulness. In truth, she did need to get away from the farm. She'd needed it for a while now. "I suppose I could use a night off. And I'm sure Meg would watch Tamela."

He raised an eyebrow. "No Tamela? Jeez, Rache, someone who doesn't know better would think you wanted me all to yourself."

Okay. He hadn't wanted a date with her, just a night on the town. Rachel remembered how the old Matthew had needed time away from the farm and from the family. How he'd been more comfortable in a business suit than in denim and leather.

But this man wanted to be with her tonight.

Maybe they did need some time to themselves. And maybe she should've made more dates with her husband years ago. Once they'd had Tamela, they hadn't really been a couple anymore. They'd been a family.

But a family in name only. After having a daughter, Matthew had emotionally withdrawn from Rachel, though he'd still showered Tamela with love.

His voice brought her back to the present. "So what do you say?"

There was only one thing to say if she wanted to reestablish a bond with her husband.

"I'd love to," she answered, realizing only too late that her enthusiasm hardly added to the illusion that she didn't welcome Matt's presence in her life.

If she didn't want another round of heartbreak, she'd have to hold her emotions close to her chest. There wasn't any other option.

The sky darkened to a velvet-blush hue over Main Street as Matt and Rachel left Cleo's Diner and headed toward the Bijou Movie Palace.

As they strolled past the old church, Pioneer Square and the Mercantile Department Store, Matt took in the details of Kane's Crossing: the flower-wrapped lampposts, the quaint mom-and-pop businesses, the shaded porches with their owners resting in rocking chairs or swings.

How could he have forgotten a place like this? How could his mind have been flushed out, washed up, torn down? He couldn't understand it.

He glanced at Rachel, strolling the sidewalk beside him, her head just reaching his shoulder. She'd pulled her hair into a sleek ponytail and, instead of wearing her usual horse farm gear or summer dress, she'd donned a vest and skirt. The change was telling— from *Good Housekeeping* to *Modern Woman*. He wondered if she dressed this way in public in order to separate herself from the rest of Kane's Crossing, as if she wanted to erect the same wall that stood between her and him.

Damn, she was fascinating. Maddening. Hard to figure out.

Matt cupped the back of her neck, his fingers extending to brush over a vein. Under his touch, he could feel her pulse throbbing.

She stiffened, gazing up at him with trepidation in her gray-green eyes.

He lowered his hand and stuck it in a jeans' pocket. What had he been doing anyway? He hadn't returned to Kane's Crossing to win back a wife. All he wanted was a life—his farm and a sense of who he was. Anything more than that was dangerous, because he knew that his old self didn't fit in to Rachel's plans.

There was too much tension from his casual touch. Now was a good time to shatter it. "I've come to a decision."

"Really." Rachel looked straight ahead, her gaze locked on the absent nods of passing townsfolk.

"Well, it's not as earth-shattering as you might suspect." He paused, gathering his thoughts. "I don't know if I'll ever get my memory back, so there's no use putting off my choices. I'd like to work on the farm and leave the Louisville business to Lacey."

Rachel laughed sharply and shook her head. "Didn't we already discuss this?"

Matt bristled at her tone. They'd hardly said ten words over their meat loaf and mashed potatoes at the diner. If this was a real date, Matt doubted he'd chance asking Rachel out again.

He said, "Sure we talked about this. You were giving me the information and I was taking it in. I just want to make sure that you understand my plans. That there're no surprises."

"No surprises," she repeated.

Two women wearing halter tops and frayed shorts waved at Matt from the other side of the street. "Hey, Matthew," they said, their voices fairly dripping with Southern honey.

Matt merely nodded a greeting, wondering why they'd looked at him with such slanted eyes and suggestive smiles.

Once again, he thought about the image of a green and blue nightie, about the picture of a mysterious blond woman and the little boy.

Had he been seeing women on the side? And who was that kid in the picture with the blonde?

Matt didn't want to think about the possibilities, but they invaded his thoughts anyway.

Could he have even fathered another child with a woman who wasn't Rachel? Why else did he keep thinking about these people?

And, maybe, just maybe, Chloe Lister hadn't been the only private detective looking for the missing Matthew Shane.

Sickened by this new suspicion, Matt turned his face away from his wife.

He couldn't look at her. Not if he was as awful as he suspected.

In silence, they approached the movie palace with its massive neon marquee and stone statues marking the faded importance of the structure. Gilded frames lined color-washed posters of second-run movies, and the box office stood in the middle of it all, its bow-tied ticket seller reading a detective novel to pass the time. According to the price and time list, their movie—a revival of *Jaws*—didn't start for another twenty minutes.

They bought their tickets but, at that point, things went from bad to worse.

Down the street, three people stumbled out of the pool hall. Townsfolk crossed to the opposite sidewalk as Sonny, Junior and Mitzi hooted and hollered their way toward Matt.

Junior bellowed, "Mattie!" but was thumped in the shoulder soundly by Mitzi, the tiny tomboy.

"He don't like us anymore," she said. Then, louder, "Do ya, Mattie? You're too good for the likes of us!"

Damn. This is just what he needed.

Suddenly Rachel was by his side, her hand in the crook of his arm. "It's time to go in for the movie."

His gaze met hers. "I'm going to deal with this, Rache."

Sonny, Junior and Mitzi came closer, so close Matt could see the red haze around their irises. He could also see the movie palace's ticket seller talking a mile a minute on the phone, staring pie-eyed at the approaching mass of chaos. He'd probably called the sheriff.

The thought of more stern glares from Sam Reno just made him want to jump for joy. Fun galore.

When the motley team stopped in front of Matt, he greeted them cautiously. "Evenin'."

The trio giggled, and Mitzi grabbed Sonny's arm, evidently imitating Matt and Rachel's proper stance.

"Look at me," said Mitzi. "I'm a stuck-up, fun-stealin' prune who hates livin' in Kane's Crossing."

Rachel tensed, and Matt leaned down to whisper in her ear.

"You go on in. I'll work this out."

Rachel shook her head. "No, thanks."

Matt realized that Rachel had been putting up with this type of treatment ever since he'd been gone. The thought made him want to crash his fist into a few big mouths.

While Junior started drunkenly slurring a warped rendition of a cattle call song, Sonny said, "Damn, Mattie. Is it true what they're sayin' about your memory?"

"Yeah." Matt started guiding Rachel toward the movie house.

The brakes from a well-worn Chevy squealed to a stop in the street. A diminutive man dressed in a sheriff's uniform and a deputy's badge flew out of the vehicle, arms arched near his guns.

"I got a call from the movie house saying that you're causing some trouble, Sonny Jenks."

In the back of Matt's mind, he seemed to recall an image of this man running around with Sonny and Junior, kicking a row of lockers in high school. He shut his eyes, trying to bring the memory into focus.

Damn. He'd lost it. But he couldn't help feeling that these three good old boys had been friends. Friends of *his*.

Sonny plucked Mitzi's hand from his arm, kissed it and flung it away from him. He tipped the bill of his baseball cap and flashed a yellowed smile. "Deputy Joanson. Oooo, I'm so scairt. What are ya gonna do? Shoot your water pistols at me?"

Junior and Mitzi laughed. Rachel merely sighed and tugged Matt closer to the movie house.

Even though Deputy Joanson was still on full alert, he took the time to greet them. "Evenin', Rachel, Matt."

Rachel said, "Gary, would you mind if we went to our movie?"

He flicked a glance over to them, his attention lingering on Matt for a second longer than was polite. Deputy Joanson no doubt knew the whole amnesia story by now.

"Yeah, go on, you two. I'll take care of these menaces."

Mitzi said, "Hey, Gary. I'll bet your wife and little baby are so scairt of ya. What, do ya arrest the tyke whenever he dirties his diapers?"

"Prepare to be cuffed," said Gary, primed for action.

As much as Matt would've liked to see the trio restrained and shut up in a jail cell, it would only be a temporary solution for something he'd have to deal with later. And the next time they'd be more cantankerous, more difficult to deal with.

Matt stepped forward. "Wait. There was no trouble here, Deputy."

Sonny, Mitzi, Junior *and* Rachel all just stared at him.

Joanson relaxed a little. "They weren't harrassing you?"

"It's nothing we can't handle." Matt sauntered back to Rachel, noting the expressions of wary respect on Sonny's and Junior's faces. Mitzi had just plain narrowed her eyes at him, probably wondering what his agenda was.

"Well, thank you, Mr. and Mrs. Shane," said Joanson, seemingly disappointed in their enthusiasm for justice.

As Matt took Rachel's hand and led her into the theater, he noticed a definite lack of sarcastic jokes from the trio of terror.

He also noticed a new light in his wife's eyes.

It was almost nice, that light. Trust and interest all wrapped into one. The only drawback was a lingering shadow of doubt.

After they had settled themselves into the theater's

deserted balcony with their sodas and Milk Duds, Rachel finally spoke.

"I think you made new friends out of the old."

Matt chuckled, resting a boot on the opposite knee and doffing his hat. "I need all the friends I can get."

Rachel settled back into her plush chair. She seemed to fit in with this movie palace, with its grandiose screen, its golden trim and burgundy-papered walls. "I have to say that you handled the situation well. Luckily the Kane's Crossing sheriff's department seems to be backing you up."

"If I didn't know any better, I'd think that Sam Reno and Gary Joanson have nothing more to do than chase around Sonny and the gang."

"That's about the size of it," said Rachel, popping a chocolate-coated candy in her mouth.

The lights dimmed and the screen's heavy curtains parted.

Matt leaned over to whisper, "We're the only ones in the balcony."

She pressed the candy box into his chest, keeping him at bay. "Don't you get any horny teenager ideas."

"All right." He took the Milk Duds and grinned, letting her know that he hadn't forgotten how hormones drove a man's desires—teenager or adult.

They survived the previews without Matt making any advances, but there was something about a dark movie theater that brought his hunger for Rachel to the surface.

He snuggled his arm around her and, surprisingly, she didn't resist. In fact, as *Jaws* started, she pulled closer to him, especially when the first shark-attack victim died.

Oddly enough, Matt remembered this movie, remembered watching it on the VCR with a girl cuddled next to him. He wondered if that girl was Rachel.

That duh-duh, duh-duh music wasn't helping, either. It was reflecting his own mentality, the way he was casually, methodically pressing her closer to him.

The way he was pulling her in for a kiss.

At first, she wasn't pliant, but after a moment or so of brushing his mouth against hers, she relaxed into his embrace, opening her lips to him.

The ancient velvet-cushioned chairs creaked as Matt shifted his weight and slid over to her, the wooden armrest biting into his belly.

Ever since they'd kissed that first time—Matt's first time—he'd fantasized about her mouth, its smile-lined softness, its endless possibilities. Now, as he stroked his tongue against hers, he could taste her chocolate sweetness, feeling it becoming a part of him. It was almost as if he were absorbing her, willing her memories to seep into him.

But he needed more.

More than just kisses and whispers. He wanted promises, skin-warm commitments. He knew that making love to Rachel was the last thing they both needed, but his body was doing a damned good job of convincing him that he was wrong.

Rachel came up for air, her soft voice mingling with the movie dialogue. "What do you remember about loving me, Matt?"

He hesitated, green-blue nighties and pictures of strangers haunting his answer. "I think my body recalls everything, Rache. The information just hasn't traveled to my brain yet."

Perfect. How was that for a circular response?

But hurting Rachel with his lack of memory would only take away this new home he'd found. It could erase a blossoming relationship with a loving daughter. It could push his wife away forever.

Yet didn't he want to hold Rachel at arm's length? Didn't he want to shield her from the man who'd broken her heart in the first place? The man he used to be?

During the pause in conversation, Matt bent his head to Rachel's neck, kissing her throat, smelling her sweet perfume. He loosened her tight ponytail, feeling her jasmine-scented hair spill over his forearms.

Her hands ran over his back, under his shirt. The action drove him onward, killing his common sense. Damn, even her slight touch could heat his body to the point of near explosion.

As she nestled her knee between his legs, Matt groaned, the sound lost as he buried his face in her hair.

The movie music echoed Matt's throbbing scar, driving the pulsing beat straight down to his arousal.

When Rachel's fingers fluttered over his zipper, he grabbed her hand.

She responded by nipping at his ear, his neck. Damn, she was so responsive, so attuned to what his body wanted.

Why did he feel that they'd kissed like this for hours at a time? Why did it feel so familiar?

He whispered, "I want you, Rachel."

And he did. Even though it wasn't right.

Her answer was to lead his hand to her vest, where she undid the buttons then guided his fingers inside.

Soft skin, hot skin. He trailed a finger around the lace of her bra, running his thumb over the material covering her hardened nipple. As she smoothed her own hands over his chest, Matt dipped into her bra's cup, stroking the nipple between two fingers.

A blast of shock music ripped through the movie house, making Rachel jump. Another shark victim.

Another moment shot to hell.

As they pulled away from each other, Rachel peered around the balcony, obvious relief written on her face.

"Thank goodness we're alone," she said.

Thank goodness for a lot of things. He'd come perilously close to losing himself to his wife, something he knew was an impossibility.

As his heartbeat flooded his thoughts, Rachel eased to the far side of her seat, fanning herself. Matt took the hint and didn't touch her for the rest of the film.

Well, damn. He'd just ignore his worked-up libido and be a good boy. But that was easier said than done.

When the house lights glared over the theater at the movie's end, Rachel placed a hand on his shoulder to keep him in his seat.

"One more time, Matt. What do you remember about making love to me?"

Maybe honesty would be the best policy. "I'm not sure, Rachel."

Her hand slipped down his arm, and her eyes lost a little of their light. "I understand."

Frustration welled in his chest. "It's not that—"

"I know. Believe me, I know." She stood, adjusting her vest. The old Rachel, the proper wife with a glaze of frost, reappeared. "I suspect that all you ever wanted from me was the physical part of love. I wanted more, Matt."

But he didn't.

He'd never be able to give her his heart. It was a piece of him that still belonged to the old Matthew.

And he wasn't about to subject Rachel to that man again.

Chapter Eight

Even thinking about it a few nights later, Rachel couldn't believe she'd gone so far in the balcony of a movie theater.

As she bit her lip and got the last of dinner to carry out to the table on the dining terrace, she chastised herself. Making out in movie balconies was kid stuff. Where was the control she took such pride in?

It'd flown out her ears, right along with her common sense.

She hadn't spent a lot of time with Matt since the movies, thank goodness. Both of them had gone about their business, primarily that of avoiding each other.

Today hadn't been much different, but they couldn't get away with ignoring each other through another dinner. Especially with Tamela around.

She walked onto the covered dining terrace carrying one of Meg Cassidy's lemon meringue pies. With addle-brained inspiration, Rachel had spent extra time preparing the meal today, cooking up honey glazed ham, freshly baked rolls, green peas and salad. Maybe if she filled Matt's stomach, he wouldn't be so quick to reach for *her*.

"There you go," she said, serving the foamy slices, pasting a too-cheery smile on her face. She couldn't let Matt know how their balcony caresses had affected her, how they'd made her rethink keeping her distance from the husband who'd hurt her.

Tamela immediately dug into the pie, concentrating on cleaning her plate.

Matt, however, did no such thing. He leaned back in his chair, one booted ankle kicked carelessly over the opposite knee as he grinned. "You trying to fatten me up, Rache?"

She bit her tongue before she could say that she liked him just how he was. Long-legged, lean hipped and muscle firmed. "Meg stopped by today with a pie."

Tamela's head shot up from her plate, meringue slathered around her mouth. "They're witchy pies, Daddy."

As their daughter attacked her food once more, Matt shot a bemused glance at Rachel. "Sounds intriguing."

Obviously Matt didn't remember this little piece of Kane's Crossing gossip. "It's funny, really. People around these parts believe that Meg's baking has magical powers. 'Blueberry pie, win your guy. Angel food cake a marriage does make.'"

Matt stared at the pastry with new interest. "So what's this? A marriage-mending masterpiece?"

"Nice. You're catching on," said Rachel, sinking into her seat.

Even though Meg hadn't actually created the pie for Rachel's convenience, she wouldn't correct Matt. If he intended to stay on the farm and be a father to Tamela, they needed all the help they could get.

Tamela reached for another piece, but Matt was quicker. He grabbed her hands in his.

"Hey, brownie locks. You're going to turn into one big lemon."

"Am not," said Tamela, giggling, tugging her hands away from her father.

"I don't know," he said, narrowing his eyes and rubbing his chin between a thumb and forefinger. "Someone's getting yellow-skinned. And her mouth's starting to pucker up like this."

He imitated a lemon-juice scowl.

Both Tamela and Rachel laughed together. When was the last time the six-year-old had been so happy?

As the little girl jumped up from her seat and bounded onto her daddy's lap, Rachel felt her heart squeeze itself dry.

Tamela loved her father. Every day presented a new reminder of this fact.

Could Rachel live with this man? True, he brought

occasional joy to their lives, but... What if the old Matthew showed up one day, his memories intact, his love for his family relegated once again to the back burner?

How would Tamela react if her daddy went back to his workaholic grind? His stay-out-late shenanigans?

Tamela and Matt had lapsed into a game of paper/rock/scissors to see who had the honor of clearing the table.

As Matt's paper covered Tamela's rock, the child giggled. "No, you have to help me."

He pretended to think about it, then winked at Rachel. "Promise to read me a story tonight?"

"Okay," said the child, even though Matt would actually do the storytelling.

"Good."

Matt prepared to lift Tamela off his lap, but their daughter caught him off guard.

With a burst of energy, she threw her slight arms around his neck, squeezing him to her. "I love you, Daddy."

Rachel swallowed the lump in her throat, touched. She, herself, hadn't even shown Matt this much innocent affection since his return. Why was it so easy for her daughter to accept him again?

Matt caught her eye, and she knew that he was thinking the same thing. Slowly he pulled back from Tamela.

"What do you say we clear this table?" he asked.

His voice was scratchy, as if it'd been damaged—yet reshaped—by years of hard winds.

Tamela, seemingly unaware of the tense emotions hovering between the adults, jumped down from her father's lap and grabbed some silverware. "I can carry more than you."

Rachel cleared her throat, banishing her emotions. "Slow down, Tam. We've got all night."

Matt's gaze heated, flushing Rachel's skin from her forehead to her toes.

As the young girl left the terrace, Rachel knew she'd chosen the wrong words.

Yes, they had all night. And from the expression on Matt's face, he wanted to take advantage of it.

She didn't know if she could fight their desire anymore.

After they cleaned up the kitchen and tucked Tamela into bed, Rachel disappeared.

Matt knew she probably needed time to herself, and he should allow her the opportunity to gather her thoughts, especially after their movie date.

Damn. He couldn't even think straight himself when it came to Rachel. All he could concentrate on these past few days as he'd visited the city doctors for more head tests and worked with the horses was Rachel's soft skin, her misty eyes, her slim curves.

Even if he couldn't remember much from his past, he was building memories day by day. Powerful memories.

But why wasn't that enough?

He knocked on her bedroom door. No answer.

Where was she? He'd checked almost every room. Her car was even still in the garage.

A thought kicked in. Over a week ago, when he'd walked the property, he'd been drawn to a quaint garden house close to the main building. Could Rachel have gone there? It wouldn't hurt to check.

As he walked over the night-cool grass, his rib scar began to ache. He felt empty inside, devoid of something integral to his existence. Maybe finding Rachel would ease that numb ache.

Filmy blue curtains breezed out from the massive open windows of the garden house as Matt approached. Large creamy flowers bloomed around the surrounding terra-cotta tiles and the vine-covered wooden posts. Pine gazebo lanterns shed a glow over the landscape as he lightly knocked on the door.

He could hear someone stirring inside. Then "Yes?"

Her tone was whisper soft, throaty. His heart and his scar pounded together, connected by his need to be with her.

"It's the Big Bad Wolf. I need to borrow some sugar."

During the ensuing pause, he could hear strains of sad radio music lilting over the summer air.

She finally spoke. "Come in."

He pushed open the door, his eyes adjusting to the dim lantern light. The room was sparsely decorated, housing a table laden with a portable radio and knitting needle-impaled yarn skeins; clay pots dotted the floor, filled with delicate, aromatic plants. On a white wicker-boarded bed lay Rachel, cuddled into the pillows, her dress pooled around her body, knitting needles and a half-finished sweater spread out next to her. Pink tear stains streaked down her cheeks.

Matt felt as if he'd invaded a hideaway. "I can talk with you later."

She sighed and leaned on an elbow. "You caught me."

"Doing what?" As if he needed to ask. She'd been crying. And Matt had the sneaking suspicion that he'd been the cause of it.

"What was I doing? I come here when I need to gather my head together. It's another world, but still close enough to hear Tam if she needs me." Then, with an embarrassed shrug, she indicated the yarn. "I guess I can't hide my old-maid side any longer, huh?"

"You don't seem the knitting type."

Rachel smiled, her eyelids drooping over the cloudy-water hue of her gaze. "It's relaxing. Puts me right to sleep."

Matt took a chance and stepped nearer to her. She didn't flee. Didn't even seem frantic that he was near.

Was she more comfortable with him now?

The smooth-as-sherry voice of Patsy Cline wafted between them, interrupted by that of the deejay. He announced the continuation of the Sweet Dreams request hour "after these words from our sponsors."

Rachel removed the knitting items to the ground and patted the bed. "You might as well sit. I'm feeling guilty, making you be all polite and proper when we've been married for years."

Tentatively Matt took a seat on the bed, feeling the mattress dip under his weight. "I made you cry, didn't I?"

"Not you." She drew a circle on the bedspread with a forefinger, watching the pattern intently. "It's just everything. I needed to get my head together in here."

Matt smoothed back a strand of hair that had blocked her gaze. Her eyes met his.

She said, "Do you think we can work out this marriage?"

There it was. The question he'd been dreading. The question he'd been wishing for. Even though he'd spent hours thinking about the answer, he still didn't know how to respond.

The picture of the woman and child. The nightie.

There was still too much he didn't understand about his old self.

He took a deep breath, then blew it out. "I think all we can do is take it one day at a time, Rache."

Her answering laugh was tinged with melancholy. "I shouldn't have expected a fairy-tale solution." She paused. "You probably don't remember anything about my childhood, but I was so serious. A lot like

Tamela, sometimes. Late at night, after my parents would exchange those nightly cold shoulders, I'd hide in my room, wishing someone would come in to tell me a story. To spend some time with me.''

Matt's gut twisted. He could imagine a stoic young Rachel, taking on the weight of the world, just like she'd done for the past two years.

Since she hadn't retreated when he'd touched her hair, he tried again. This time he stroked from her forehead to her neck, his touch slow and steady, gentle as a heat-hushed night.

He said, "Tamela's lucky that she has a mother who'll give her all the love and attention she wants.''

"And a father, right?" Rachel leaned her head toward his hand, and he cupped his palm and fingers against her scalp, massaging.

She said, "Up in that hideaway room, I used to change the endings of the fairy tales. They always ended up so sadly.''

"Why?"

She smiled up at him, a quivering hint of pain. "I didn't know any better. There weren't exactly happy endings in my household.''

Before he could ask another question, Rachel leaned over to brush her lips against his wrist. Her warm mouth shot a blast of desire through his veins, and he gently bunched his fingers in her hair.

"Dammit, I can't stay away from you, Rachel," he said.

What a jerk I am, he thought. They'd received the

results of his STD tests today—negative—but even that good news didn't mean Rachel would sleep with him.

But he couldn't help the longing for her. It overwhelmed his common sense, overshadowed his better instincts.

"Shh," she said, pulling him all the way onto the bed until his body stretched along hers. She sat up and shucked off his boots, hearing the muted thump, thump as they hit the floorboards. "Let's not talk right now."

Because talking would shatter the serenity of this cricket-thick evening. It would tear down the curtains wisping back and forth in the breeze. It would cover the bass, the piano and the violins swirling together with Patsy Cline's barely restrained heartache.

Instead, as Matt settled on his back, Rachel curled into him. She rested her head on his chest, snuggled a bent leg between his knees, rested a palm over the drumbeat of his heart. She breathed in the scent of saddle leather and soap, the smell of the new Matt soothing her wounded memories.

She wished they could stay like this forever, wrapped up in each other, fitted together so nothing— not even doubt—could separate them.

If they never had to talk again, their marriage could be repaired.

She listened to the quietude, to the uneven tempo of his breathing. Since she always left Tamela's window open in case her daughter needed her, her ears were constantly tuned in to any sounds.

"Rachel," said Matt, skimming his lips over her ear.

The wet-warm contact shook her steady pulse. Though her mind only wanted to cuddle, her body wanted something more. Much more.

She rubbed against his thigh, drawing her fingers over his ribs.

She'd obviously encouraged him, because he rolled them both over, molding himself to her, his mouth covering hers with long, slow kisses.

She melted into them, parting her lips to allow his tongue entrance, moaning quietly.

Careful, softly, she told herself. Even small sounds would carry on the summer air.

What was she doing anyway? Hadn't she just berated herself for making out with Matt in a movie theater? True, she and Matthew had once mastered the art of marathon kissing, but...

He slipped his hand under her dress and between her legs. She put her own hand over his, pressing harder, guiding him.

"There," she whispered, arching against his touch, her body aching.

As he circled his thumb over her panties, she felt years of pressure building, her blood pumping and flowing to the tender spot he was massaging. As she moved with the swirl of his touch, she hurled along an endless explosion roaring with emotion.

It'd been so long since she'd made love with Matthew. How was she going to stop herself?

She couldn't stop herself.

Rachel's breaths came in gasps, her body heating from the inside out, as she shifted against him, pushing him to his back, straddling him. In her urgency, she ripped open his denim shirt, sending buttons flying.

He grinned. "I suppose we needed more rags in the barn anyway."

She almost said she was sorry, but didn't bother.

No apologies, just skin. Warm skin, sweat coating her chest and stomach and legs as she parted his shirt and ran her hands over his chest.

"I missed this," she whispered.

Matt watched her with that encouraging half smile. "I'm pretty sure I did, too," he said, smoothing his palms up her belly, her rib cage.

As he moved higher and traced his thumbs around the hardened tips of her breasts, Rachel caught her breath. "We have to be quiet. Tam's window—"

The words caught in her throat when he trailed his fingers down the center of her stomach, down her belly, rubbing them over the front of her panties again.

His chuckle rankled her, excited her.

She whispered, "I think I hate you, Matt Shane."

"Keep right on hating me then."

Good advice, she thought, ignoring the consequences for making love to her own husband.

She slipped her dress over her head, tossing it to the floor, then wiggled out of her bra while Matt watched and eased a thumb tip in and out of her belly button.

Almost naked, almost totally vulnerable in front of the man who'd hurt her time and again. Was she an idiot?

Rachel covered her breasts with crossed arms, suddenly shy with the lanterns' glow spotlighting her. Then she remembered her underwear.

Too late. Matt had already looked.

He chuckled again. "Why, Grandma. What big undies you have."

He tucked a thumb into the thick waistband and snapped it back.

He'd always made fun of her underwear whether he realized it or not. She wondered if he remembered.

She shrugged farther into the protection of her crossed arms. "All right," she said softly. "So they leave a lot to the imagination. They're comfortable, okay?"

Matt folded his arms under his head and leaned back. "This, from a woman who dresses to the nines, even when she's wearing jodhpurs. Who would've guessed?"

His opened shirt had parted even more, showcasing the gleam of sweat-slicked chest muscles. A pale streak ran between two ribs, catching her eye.

She reached out to touch it. "What's this?"

Matt's eyes darkened. Without another word, he sat

up, lightly pushing her back onto the mattress. He coaxed her arms away from her chest, spreading them above her head, allowing the air to blow over her damp, exposed skin.

Then he bent to cover one nipple with his mouth, and Rachel squirmed beneath his weight. As he swirled his tongue up, over and around, she wrapped a leg around the back of his thigh, urging him closer.

His arousal was clear, outlined by the bulge in his jeans. The radio music became hazy, an angel's voice floating over the rhythm of their movements.

She wanted more. Rachel shifted her hips, just as the wind changed direction and blew the curtains over their bodies. The soft flutter of the sheer material beat against her thigh.

She could feel him straining against her, could feel his hardness pressing between her legs.

He trailed kisses over her skin, licking the underside of her breasts, running his lower lip over every rib on the way down to her belly. He grazed his teeth over her trembling stomach, and she fought the urge to stroke her nails over his shoulders.

As he pulled her undies down her legs, she could feel his breath skim over the very center of her. On his way back up, he used his lips and tongue to explore her calves, her inner thighs. When he loved her with his mouth, Rachel gasped, biting her lip until she tasted blood.

She was ready for him, sleek and heated, buzzing for him to be inside of her.

He slid up her body with his own, skin on skin, and kissed her neck. "Will you regret this?"

Of course she would, but she didn't give a damn. "Just take off your jeans, Matt."

Grinning, he stood, shucking his pants to the floor.

This is how it'd been when they'd taken the Seville honeymoon. This is why they'd gotten married in the first place. Because they couldn't keep their hands off each other.

Because neither of them had thought about the ramifications.

But it didn't matter. She was a big girl now.

He came back to her, every bit of him unclothed. As he stretched over her body, she shivered, loving the feel of the sparse hairs on his legs, on his chest. Loving how the slight roughness scratched against her bare skin.

His length nudged against her leg, against her heat. She ran a palm over him, flushing all over when he groaned. She led him into her, drawing in a breath at the way he filled her. It was as if a missing piece had been given back, as if she'd been waiting over two years to find completion.

They moved together, and she rested her mouth against the vein in his throat, feeling the throb of his pulse. It echoed hers, overlapping her own heartbeat, creating an answering rhythm.

In this isolated world, she knew everything about him. She knew how he liked his eggs cooked in the morning. She knew how a perfect sunset could make him choke on words. She knew how her jasmine perfume used to make him tear off her clothing.

She knew how they'd never been able to resist each others' bodies.

Matt stiffened, climaxing with a shudder, then relaxed against her, taking care to see that she was just as fulfilled. He pleasured her until she sobbed for breath, until the world rotated around in a whirl of colors, whizzing by with the speed of a spinning gun barrel. Then that world burst to a stop, making Matt the center of her ecstasy.

He cupped her face in his hands, tracing his thumbs along her jawline. "I thought you weren't coming back from wherever you just went," he said quietly.

Rachel swallowed, still reeling, her breathing evening out. She couldn't answer, could only skim back the damp hank of hair that continually loitered over his forehead.

From the corner of her gaze, she saw the pale scar slashed between his ribs.

Yes, she'd sure come back. And with a vengeance.

And he'd come back, too. Back to Kane's Crossing.

Now it was time to find out where he'd been.

Chapter Nine

Matt peered down at his wife as he braced an arm on either side of her body.

In the lantern light, her skin glowed with the sheen of beaded sweat. Her breasts rose and fell with every breath, making him want to taste her again. And again.

She was everything he'd hoped for, and more.

Right now she was watching him, probably because she thought he'd remember something about their old relationship. Well, he didn't. And he couldn't say he was unhappy about it.

She ran a finger over his scar, causing him to flinch. "Where'd you get this, Matt?"

He tried to laugh off the question. "What, don't all men have one? It started with Adam, you know."

She sighed, using a fingernail to trace his scar. He clenched his jaw and hoped she'd let it pass.

"You never said anything about this injury, Matt. You came clean about your head wounds, but this—" she pressed her palm against his heart "—this is something new."

Matt had known that Rachel would see his scar sooner or later. He'd just been hoping that it'd be later. He hadn't expected them to fall into bed, victims of their raging libidos.

Would he lie to her about this? It didn't seem to be a good option, especially since they'd just made love, been intimate, shared more than cautious glances.

If he wanted to start a new life and forget the old Matthew, he'd have to tell the truth.

He helped her to a sitting position, removing her hand from his flesh. She fisted the bedspread and covered herself with it. Feeling oddly vulnerable, he followed her gesture.

They were almost strangers again.

He ran his fingertips over the pucker of his wound, trying to draw a memory from it. But touching it had never worked. Why did he think it'd work now?

"Rache?" He smoothed a wet strand of hair away from her eyes. "I'm not sure how I got the scar."

She turned away from his hand, and he balled it into a fist, lowering it.

She said, "You know more than you're telling me. Was it from the night you lost your memory?"

He hesitated, wondering how much he should tell her, then nodded. "I'm not going to lie to you. I'm just not sure what happened."

"Well, thank goodness untruths are off-limits."

"Hell, Rachel, all I have control of are lies. How will it sound when I tell you that I woke up with my head pounding and blood on my hands?"

She pulled away slightly. The added distance was subtle, but meant everything to Matt.

She said, "Blood? From the rib wound, right?"

Damn, what could he say? That he might've inflicted just as much damage on the person who'd stabbed *him?* "I know Matthew—I—wasn't the perfect husband."

She lowered her gaze.

He cursed under his breath, then continued. "I'll tell it to you straight. I was bleeding from a cut on the left side of my rib cage. But...on the other side of my shirt, the side with no injuries, I had a circle of blood. It was smeared down my pants, too. Nowhere near my own wound. I couldn't figure out how the blood had gotten there."

Rachel shot a glare at him. "Are you saying it was someone else's blood?"

"I'm saying that I don't know."

Silence roared over the room. Then Rachel stood, wrapping the bedspread around her body. She started pacing, running her fingers through her hair in obvious agitation. "Matthew, what did you do?"

The other man's name shot through him, ripping

away some of the healing he thought had taken place. "I have no idea. But maybe I need to be the one asking questions, Rachel. Everyone tiptoes around me, holding back information about the man I used to be. Do you think it's helping? Is it doing any good at all?"

She turned to him, anger reddening her skin. "Okay. You want to hear all about it? Well, here we go.

"You stayed away from the farm like it was the plague, and I have no idea why. We had a great sex life, but you can already guess that much, I'm sure. We fell out of love, Matt. I even wondered—"

She cut herself off.

"What?" he asked, rising from the bed.

"Nothing." She started glancing around, then grabbed her dress off the floor, tugging it over her head. When she couldn't get one arm through a sleeve, she cursed, trying harder. After a few strained seconds, she gave up, sinking to a chair, sobbing.

Matt wrapped a sheet around his lower half, then reached out to her. He stopped before he touched her, clenching his fingers until his nails burned into his palms. He'd guessed that his wife had been hurt by him in the past, but he hadn't known the extent of it.

Damn Matthew Shane. Every day he hated the man more.

Softly he said, "Do you think Matthew could've injured someone like that?"

She gazed up at him, her head in her hands, tears

trembling on her eyelashes. "You talk about him as if he's another person."

Matt wondered if he was. But if the old Matthew came back with his memory...

"You didn't answer me," he said.

She stared at him for a moment, then shook her head. "Matthew did a good job of wounding me. What do you think he could've done to someone else?"

Matt had a bad feeling that the other man could've been capable of spilling another person's blood. Problem was, he *was* the other man.

The next morning a distracted Rachel emerged from her study after fiddling with the account books, then headed outside.

She hated being cooped up in the office, deprived of fresh air and time to think about what she'd done with Matt last night.

Obsessing about their lovemaking was far easier than remembering his scar and the lack of explanation that went along with its pale anger.

Was Matthew capable of shedding someone else's blood? He'd never been violent, and his temper had always been controlled, so the whole story didn't make sense.

Rachel wanted to talk with Chloe, to see if the private investigator had unearthed any more information about Matthew's time in New Orleans. Maybe the detective could put her mind at ease. Or maybe she could make matters worse with her findings.

At any rate, Rachel needed to know the truth. If Matthew had crossed a line during his absence, she didn't want him around Tamela, or around her.

Or should she just send Matt away until they learned what he'd done?

But would that be fair to any of them?

She walked over to a shaded clump of elm trees and sat on a large rock overlooking the horse farm. Her judgment had certainly gone down the tubes. Even if last night's lovemaking hadn't awakened Tamela, it was still ill advised, especially after her newfound doubts about her husband.

Instinct forced her to look over her shoulder, just as she'd done the first day Matt had come home. And there he was, sauntering along with jeans-and-leather ease, a pair of work gloves hanging from one hand while the other hand tipped up his Stetson.

"Hey," he said, his tone a casual Texas drawl. "I thought I saw you up here hiding again."

Last night's argument provided a wall between them, but she wanted to knock it down. She'd spent her entire life keeping secrets, talking around matters until they littered her soul with everyone else's pain. Deep inside, her mother's mistakes still lingered, as did her own shortcomings as Matthew's wife.

"I've been thinking that maybe you should leave," she blurted.

She could tell that Matt was forcing himself to not

react. The lines around his mouth deepened, the half smiles around his eyes all but disappeared.

"Because of what I told you last night. Right?"

Rachel tucked a strand of loose hair back into her braid. "Right. If you developed a violent streak during the last two years, I don't want you around Tamela."

Matt shifted his stance, resting his weight on one leg while slapping the gloves against the other. He glared at the ground, then looked up, the slow burn of his eyes marking her. "How many times do I need to tell you that I'm not the old Matthew?"

"But you are." She stood. "It's just a matter of time until you remember what you did to earn that scar."

"Don't you think I know that?" he asked. "It's been pressing down on me since I got back. I can see how you look at me with questions in your eyes. I also see how much Tamela needs a father. Now, I can't prove my innocence, but I guess I just need for you to trust me."

Trust. It was one thing she'd never had enough of.

"How can you ask me to put my faith in you, Matthew?"

His jaw muscles flexed, then he whipped the Stetson off his head, flinging it toward the grass. At the last moment, he pulled back, probably realizing that his aggression wouldn't help his case. He held up his hands in the air.

"I know I'm asking for the impossible," he said.

"Then don't ask anymore," she whispered, thinking of her mother and the many times she'd deceived her family. Thinking of the old Matthew and all the ways he'd broken her heart.

Rachel had forgotten that yesterday, after they'd received the news of his clean bill of health, she'd actually cherished the resulting surge of trust, the relief. But now, knowing about the scar, she had no reason to have faith in him. No reason at all.

Matt stood silently for a moment, his gaze fixed beyond Rachel. Then softly he said, "I just want a home."

The sentiment pierced her heart. What did she think he was going to do? Stalk his wife and child in the middle of the night with a knife? Sure, this man was a stranger, but he'd also contributed to the birth of Tamela. He'd married Rachel and given her a few years of extreme joy before distancing himself.

Rachel twisted the wedding ring on her finger, trying to force a decision. Time seemed to hang over them, waiting to swoop down, to feed off their fragile bond.

Matt's soft voice cut through her musing. "I guess we didn't splurge on the ring, did we?"

She glanced at the silver band engraved with connecting roses and thorns, and smiled slightly, relieved to be talking about something other than last night. "It was the most beautiful piece of jewelry I'd ever seen. After college, we went to Madrid, and we were walking through a street market when I saw it. You had a lot of money from your parents, and you wanted to buy me a huge diamond ring for our engagement. But I·wanted this—something simple, elegant, meaningful.'' She paused. ''I never wanted anything more.''

He walked closer, hesitated, then stepped nearer again. She tentatively held out her hand so he could take a better look.

He said, ''When I first saw this ring, as Matt, not Matthew, I had a few impressions. I think I knew it was from Spain.'' He paused. ''I also wondered if you'd worn that ring just as faithfully as intended. Or if you'd taken it off when you were with other men while I was gone.''

He was asking if she'd slept around. The stubborn side of her refused to reveal that she'd been as constant as steel, as hopeful as the sun rising over a dark world.

She couldn't give him the satisfaction of certainty, especially if her doubts about Matthew proved true.

''We went back to Spain on our honeymoon,'' she said instead, avoiding his intimate question. ''To Seville.''

He looked away, and Rachel had the feeling he was just as willing as she to ignore their troubles for the moment.

He said, ''Isn't it strange how I remember something so useless?''

Rachel shook her head, her shoulders relaxing.

"It's not insignificant, Matt. In fact, Seville meant everything. We were very much in love back then."

And they could still be now, she thought. If she could trust him. If she could forget about everything the other Matthew had done.

Last night they'd made love with the fervor and heat of their honeymoon days, but she didn't want to tell him that.

"Matt," she began, then turned away. Had she actually made a decision about letting him be a part of her and Tamela's lives?

"I'm listening, Rache," he said.

That much was true. This new Matt paid attention to her, made her feel desired again. He'd even offered a vague feeling of safety before she'd found out about the scar last night.

But what did the wound actually mean? Wasn't it merely circumstantial evidence? Couldn't he have lain in his *own* blood and stained the other side of his shirt?

Was it enough to deprive Tamela of a father?

She exhaled, wondering if she was making the right choice. "I'll allow you to be around Tamela, but I want to be there at the same time. All right?"

He clenched his jaw while a mocking smile strained over his mouth. Then he said, "I guess that's warranted."

She twisted her ring again. "And also, don't expect last night to repeat itself."

He lifted an eyebrow, and Rachel knew she'd injured him. That poker-tell brow just meant he wasn't about to make an issue of it.

She stumbled over her words in haste, wanting to make sure he knew what to expect. Or what to not expect.

"I wasn't thinking clearly last night, Matt, because if I had been, I'd have known that having sex would just complicate matters."

The brow was still raised. She knew what was probably running through his mind: a miffed stream of consciousness in which he wondered why she'd called it "sex" instead of "making love."

He was such an awful poker player.

She continued. "We should've given each other space until you've had more time to adjust. And I shouldn't have misled you into thinking that our marriage would be improved by working it out in the sack."

God, she sounded callous. But how else could she get across her point?

Falling in love—or anything close to it—was dangerous. And if last night had been any indication, she wasn't too far from loving him again.

"Duly noted," he said. "Let me clarify. Basically I'm just a stranger passing through your life while you agonize over your old husband, hoping I don't hocus-pocus back into him."

"That's not what I meant at all."

Matt jammed the hat back on his head. "Just for the record, let me tell you something. I can't stand the thought of Matthew. Any guy who'd treat you and Tamela the way he did deserves what he got in New Orleans.''

He chopped out a laugh. "I can't believe I'm talking about myself this way. But that's how it is. And frankly I don't want to be that man again.''

"What if you can't help it?'' Rachel asked. "What if you can't leave the old Matthew behind?''

"I will, Rachel.'' He pointed a finger in the air, emphasizing his determination. "I damn sure will.''

When he walked away, toward the breeding barn, Rachel fought the hope that had invaded her heart.

Because she was pretty sure, at some point, the old Matthew *would* come back.

For good.

Over the days, Rachel and Matt kept their promises. He spent time with Tamela, and Rachel was always there watching. They didn't sleep together. They merely played at being a family, and it was taking its toll on Rachel's nerves.

Then P.I. Chloe Lister called with news. Bad news.

Rachel had the cordless phone in her room, pacing the floor. "Chloe, can't we piece this together? I know we mistook another man for Matt a couple months back when he was using my husband's credit cards, but that's because the wallet was lodged for two years behind those old crates in the alley where he was attacked. The man said that he'd been helping to move the business's belongings when he found the I.D. and cards.''

"Right," said Chloe. "And we know that the business he was helping to move was a ramshackle bar. Meaning that Matt was in a pretty seedy area when he was attacked.''

"Okay." Rachel bunched the material of her dress in a fist, knowing that Chloe was working up to even worse news. She could feel it coming. "So what's this all leading to?''

"I'm just adding to the information we already have. Remember the two hundred thousand dollars he withdrew from your bank account?''

"Right." Rachel and Matt had argued about it again the other night. She'd been trying to get him to tell her what he'd done with it, but he hadn't been able to. Mainly she'd been frustrated with the farm, and two hundred thousand dollars would've gone a long way in helping them.

Chloe sighed on her end of the line. "You're not going to like this.''

"Just give it to me," said Rachel, thinking that nothing could be worse than what she'd endured already.

"I know what he did with the money. I just don't know who he did it with and why he did it.''

Suddenly Rachel didn't want to hear any more.

But Chloe was already speaking. "I've talked with some people who tell me that Matthew was using the money to pay off another man.''

Rachel plunked down on her bed. "What man?"

Chloe paused. "I'm not sure. Yet. But I'll find out."

Things were going from bad to worse. "I..." Rachel choked on her own tear, unable to continue the conversation. "Thank you, Chloe."

And, without waiting for an answer, Rachel hung up the phone, sapped of strength.

And trust.

Chapter Ten

When Rachel slumped into the family room that night, the cuckoo clock struck seven, demanding Matt's attention.

She clutched a phone in one hand, her knuckles a skeletal shade of white. Red circles haunted her eyes, emphasizing now-pale skin. "Two hundred thousand dollars, Matt. What the hell could you have done with it?"

Luckily Tamela was in her room playing music and drawing, so they were safe to hash things out. Again.

Matt set down his newspaper, leaned forward in his seat and shoved his fingers through his hair, making another effort to reach into his memory. He wanted to give her the answers they needed, but the information wouldn't surface.

Useless. "Was that Chloe?" he asked instead.

Rachel must've realized that spearing him with more questions was fruitless. She tossed the phone onto the couch, then sank into the cushions, exhaling. In a nutshell, she told Matt about the private detective's news.

She asked, "You can't remember anything about that night? Not even after hearing this tidbit?"

The faint stench of acrid smoke and a sense of desperation washed over his senses. Matt tried to grab on to the sensation, but it fled before he could comprehend its meaning.

"Dammit," he muttered, shoving himself out of the chair. He was tired of disappointing everyone with his lack of understanding. Tired of making Rachel's life hell.

She rubbed a hand over her forehead, shutting her eyes. "I know. It'll take time. You might not ever remember anything."

Matt's laugh grated the air. Leaving Matthew behind sounded like a good idea to him.

He slowly paced the room, frustrated. With every passing day, the old Matthew resurfaced a little more. A flash of memory here, a clue from Chloe there. Matthew Shane was doing his best to come between Matt and Rachel, that was for sure.

He came to a stop before the French doors. The view stretched from one dimly lit end of Kane's Crossing to the other.

This was Matthew's territory. Not his.

And the old Matthew was probably doing him and Rachel a favor by wedging them apart. After all, Matt didn't want to find himself in the position of hurting his wife and child once again.

The only way to keep his family safe from the bad man he used to be was to resist falling back in love with Rachel. To resist hurting her again.

Little footsteps thumped down the stairs. Tamela's voice followed. "Mommy, Daddy, see what I made?"

She flew into the room, brown curls bouncing while she held a crayon-bright picture in front of her. "See?"

Rachel donned a strained smile, spreading out her arms to welcome her daughter. "Show us, honey."

She took the picture, then hesitated. When Matt moved to her side, he saw the reason for her silence.

Tamela had drawn a house, a horse, a tree and three happy stick people with ridiculously huge smiles. The child stood between the parents, and they all held hands.

An overwhelming feeling of horror seared into him, blinding his sight into a field of hot-pale pain. His scar throbbed, adrenaline spilling through him, jamming his heart up his throat.

"Matt?" It was Rachel.

He evened out his breathing. "I'm all right. Just… God."

The family, together, happy. This wasn't his wife

and child. It could never be, because Matthew had already destroyed the possibility.

He must've been staring into space because, when a concerned Rachel and Tamela came back into focus, Rachel asked, "Did you take your antiseizure medication?"

He couldn't tell her about his reaction to the picture. "Yeah, Nurse Rachel."

Tamela peered up at her mom, owl-eyed. "Is Daddy okay?"

Rachel turned to him, and he knew exactly what was running through her mind.

No, Daddy was not okay.

"He's fine, Tam," she said, standing and holding out a hand to their daughter. "Bedtime for the budding artist."

As she headed toward the steps, Tamela in tow, Rachel was the epitome of control. Her summer dress was crisp and proper, her voice cool and precise. Over her shoulder, she said, "Matt? Tomorrow night we have to put in an appearance at Peter Tarkin's art reception. In and out, like good business partners."

What, did she think his short-term memory had failed as well? "I know, Rachel."

She nodded and, for just a moment, Matt thought he saw a flash of concern soften her gaze. "Just thought I'd remind you. Good night."

With that, she led Tamela upstairs.

Matt couldn't subdue another rise of fear in his

chest as he watched mother and daughter holding hands, just like in Tamela's picture.

The only thing missing was the daddy.

The next night Rachel and Matt drove under a canopy of stars to Peter Tarkin's art reception.

They'd dressed in their best: she, in a fashionable red cocktail sheath with her hair swept up in a chignon; he, minus the cowboy hat in dressy boots, dark jeans, a dark jacket and a bolo tie over a button-down.

He'd refused to wear any of Matthew's old clothes, and Rachel couldn't be happier. The closeted garments would've been a sharp reminder of the parties and late-night work hours of the past. She needed to get to the future as fast as she could.

Matt's sable-brown hair flapped in the breeze from the Cadillac's open window. He carelessly leaned an elbow on the sill, his fingertips perched near the rear-view mirror.

Every time Rachel glanced at him her heart jittered, almost like an involuntary shudder. All she wanted to do was forget about the two hundred thousand dollars and its baggage. She wanted to comb her fingers through his cowlick-flopped hair, to relive the passion of that garden-house night.

She sighed, straightened her sheer wrap and peered out the windshield at the country road with its moon-gleamed white fences and wildflower-spangled grass.

Just keep your emotions in a safe place, she thought. Keep your cards close to your heart.

Matt glanced at her, then back at the road. "I really don't want to dance around Tarkin tonight."

Rachel shrugged. "He won't talk about business in his home, not when he could spend all his time bragging about his art collection."

"He collects more than paintings, doesn't he?"

She grinned at him. "Are you referring to Daisy Cox, his beauty queen fiancée? Matt, how astute of you."

He chuckled. "Hey, I may be partially blank, but half of my brain is still functioning."

The comment sucked the oxygen right out of the car.

Rachel struggled to regain the fleeting civility between them. "All the same, you're right about Tarkin. Daisy adds prestige to his life."

Tension echoed between them. She didn't want to go on hating him, always wondering about what he'd done. Why couldn't they move past it?

No. A better question would be: Why couldn't *she* move past it?

Matt tapped his fingers on the steering wheel. "Listen, I was trying to work some things out in my mind. As usual, right? But...the way I reacted to Tamela's family picture yesterday..."

The moment flashed into her mind: Matt's skin going white, his lips pulling themselves into a line as tight as his scar, his eyes glazing over into that ten-mile stare. She'd wondered herself what had happened to make him react so strangely.

"Go on," she said.

Matt shifted and ran a finger between his neck and his collar. "Is there any reason I'd be—I don't know—affected by Tamela's picture?"

Rachel shook her head. "I don't know, Matt. How did you feel? Sad, happy? You didn't look too healthy."

He clenched his jaw, then said, "I was scared out of my mind."

God. She almost wished he hadn't been so forthcoming with her. "I'm not sure if that's a good or bad sign. On one hand, maybe you got in touch with Matthew's emotions. But that would mean—"

"That he was afraid of you and Tamela?"

She had to turn this over in her mind. Why would she and their daughter scare him?

Rachel averted her eyes, watching the scenery from the passenger's window instead of facing Matt. In the near distance of a field, she could see the glimmer of parked cars, the twinkle of a thousand lights.

"Look," she said, pointing. "That's just off the Spencers' old property. I wonder…"

"What?"

She was exhausted with her life, the lack of control, the stiffness and proper facade of it all.

On a whim, she turned to him. "Matt, let's ditch Tarkin's artsy-fartsy bragging session. Let's explore."

The half smile returned to his face. Rachel's breath quickened at the sight of it. Long ago, they would spend hours just driving side roads, aiming for the sunset with carefree laughter. His smile reminded her of those times.

"Hell, yeah," he said, wheeling the vehicle onto a weed-choked path, guiding it toward the pinpricks of light.

They coasted into a field that doubled as a parking lot. Gravel buckled under the tires as they eased to a stop.

Upon closer glance, Rachel realized that they were crashing a wedding reception. Draped fairy lights floated over a raised platform, on which couples danced to country music. Silk finery fluttered in the night's warm breeze while white-clothed tables balanced under a tiered wedding cake and a bevy of appetizers. Away from the activities, the lucky couple posed for pictures as the bridesmaids waited their turn, clutching their cascading bouquets. The ushers cluttered behind the photographer, passing a silver flask.

Rachel's spirits lifted. "Is it naughty to invade a wedding?"

"I'm afraid so," said Matt.

The challenge in his light brown eyes goaded her. "It's either this or Tarkin's," she said.

"Are you trying to convince me or yourself?"

His words shook her up. She'd spent a lot of her life convincing herself of one thing or another. She'd talked herself into defending her mother, talked herself into letting Matthew get away with partying hard and working too much.

She grinned, liking the fact that she could escape her life for a while, masquerading her way into another. "I believe they're expecting us."

"Then let's go."

Minutes later, they were strolling into the festivities, blending with the invited guests in their semiformal clothing. As they headed toward the beverage bar, Rachel took a deep breath.

The bartender poured liquor into plastic cups and champagne flutes.

She glanced at Matt, gauging his reaction. He seemed nonplussed, casual, as he stepped to the counter for a soda.

Thank goodness, she thought. For a minute there, she'd been afraid that the old Matthew was back, bellying on up to the bar to throw down a few blasts of whiskey.

He returned to her side, offering a glass of iced tea.

"You read my mind," she said, her heart thudding as his jacket sleeve brushed her arm.

They remained on the outskirts, Rachel feeling much too aware of his height, the power of his body.

When the band wailed into a line dance song, Rachel focused on the guests. It was much safer than thinking about Matt's muscled torso or Matt's long legs entangled with hers.

"You know what?" she asked, absently leaning closer to her husband.

He responded by running a finger over the skin covering her spine, skin left exposed by her backless dress. The touch lasted merely a moment before he pulled away.

She tried to talk around the heart in her throat. "These are Spencer relatives. I recognize a few of them from the Spenco toy factory picnic a few months ago."

"Toy factory?"

"Oh, it was shut down. Horatio Spencer, Ashlyn's dad, got into some trouble with faulty machinery. Instead of toughing out an arrest, he and his wife fled the country."

Matt finished off his soda, setting the cup on a table. "But Ashlyn's still in town."

Poor woman. Not long ago, when Sam and Ashlyn had been going through their own troubles, Rachel had merely been a supporting player, listening to Sam's point of view. That had been before Matt returned, before her own personal crisis.

She said, "The Spencers betrayed Ashlyn. Sam and Taggert are her family now, and she's much better off, frankly. Horatio and Chad Spencer hurt a lot of people in Kane's Crossing."

An elderly couple strolled past them, frowning, whispering to each other.

"Uh-oh," said Matt, clearly enjoying the thought of being discovered. "Don't we fit in?"

Rachel took a long swig of her iced tea, intending to enjoy it before they were kicked out. The Spencer family—extended or not—didn't like her, especially since she'd been so supportive of Meg and Nick Cassidy, the family enemies.

She said, "I love this. Spencers on the fringes of Kane's Crossing. They don't look so powerful now."

The elderly couple had done a U-turn and was making a beeline for Matt and Rachel. Then, sent from diva heaven itself, Patsy Cline's voice washed over the air.

Rachel grinned, momentarily closing her eyes under the music's soothing bass beat. When she opened them, the man had his hand up, his mouth open.

"I say, are you—"

"Dancing," said Matt, finishing the man's sentence, grabbing Rachel's drink and fitting it into the man's hand. He cupped Rachel's elbow and led her toward the platform.

"Smooth operator," said Rachel, peering up at her husband as he ushered her up the platform steps and through the box-stepping dancers.

"I'm occasionally useful," he said, his voice lowered to a still-of-the-night hum.

They faced each other, and Rachel knew he was feeling the same trepidation. They were afraid to touch each other again.

Heck, she thought. They had to come to terms at some point.

She assumed the dancing position, arms outstretched, one hand on his broad shoulder, the other clasped in his grip. Matt got the hint and settled his palm over her hip, his fingers lightly resting on the bare small of her back.

Rachel contained a shiver of desire, fighting the need to sidle closer to his soap-and-leather scent. "Shall we?" she asked.

The ballad "Sweet Dreams" stretched between their bodies, a living heat pulsing with longing and humidity-steamed tension. Rachel was careful to leave a safe space between them, careful to see that her hand didn't relax and slide down his shoulder, careful to make sure she didn't catch his gaze.

Because, surely, his eyes were going to talk her into something stupid. Something she'd already shared with the new Matt.

She couldn't get that close again. Absolutely not.

Even if the music and their polite contact made it seem as if there was nothing wrong, she couldn't be fooled into letting down her guard.

Matt and Matthew are one and the same, she told herself. *Don't forget that.*

His fingernails smoothed over a ridge of her exposed spine. Rachel's breasts tightened, tingling with a fierce ache.

Casually she straightened her posture while looking up at the sky. Matt's fingers pulled away at the tacit reprimand.

She said, "When I was a little girl, I used to lie on

the grass, stargazing. The sky was never as endless as it is here, without city lights.''

''There's something to be said about the country.''

Their pause grew thick with unspoken thoughts.

After a few musical beats, he broke the tension. ''You seem sad when you talk about being a little girl.''

Rachel hadn't realized that she'd talked about it that much. Was he remembering her tears when she would end a phone call with her parents? Was he remembering how she'd keep her silence after every visit to New York?

She'd never told him about her mother's activities, the times she'd sneaked in through her bedroom window—dead drunk—with her lipstick smeared and her bra in hand.

Dammit, she didn't want to think about her mom.

She tried to smile, tried to leave her pain out of the equation. ''Just dance,'' she said.

When she caught his gaze, she could've smacked herself. A whiplash-quick snap of pain flashed across his eyes and then...nothing.

She'd shut him out again. But how could she help it?

He didn't need to know about her family. All he needed was his own memory, so they could all move on to the next phase of life.

He lowered his voice. ''Maybe you'll talk about it later.''

Couldn't he get the hint? She didn't want to re-member any of it.

But his concern warmed her, made her slip a bit closer to falling for him again.

She grabbed on to a slice of reality. This wasn't the man she'd married. The real Matthew was on his way, and he'd kick the new Matt—the good Matt—right out of her life.

Rachel held back a rush of grief, the scratch of something desperate and wrong tickling her throat.

"Just dance," she repeated, wishing they could spend the rest of their lives swaying in silence to a slow song.

Chapter Eleven

She was pregnant.

Rachel stared at the thin stick that screamed "Blue! Positive!" and returned it to the packaging. It joined the first stick—the one with the same result.

It'd been days since she'd danced with her husband and over three weeks since she and Matt had made love. Morning sickness had set in a couple of days ago, and she'd started to suspect the worst. Then, when her period hadn't shown up, Rachel had grown more uncomfortable. She'd driven out of town to the next county to purchase a test. Buying it in Kane's Crossing would've set off the gossip alarm for certain, and she wanted to avoid the added inconvenience of attacking busybodies.

She sat on the closed toilet seat, head in hands. What was she going to do?

They'd spent one night together. *One damned night.* Their lovemaking had been so unexpected that she hadn't even thought of protection.

How would Matt react to her news?

Oh, God, this wouldn't be good. Even if they'd been getting along these past couple of weeks, Rachel couldn't call their union a real marriage. Heck, she hadn't taken vows with the new Matt, never even been courted by him.

She stood, restless with anxiety, and paced the bathroom tiles. *You idiot, you moron, you thoughtless hormonally explosive nerd.*

She'd have to tell Matt. There was no way around it. But was it safe to give him this news? Would it scare him away? Would it unleash those damned memories?

Fear froze Rachel in her footsteps. A gut-wrenching sense of numbness made her want to run from all her problems.

Years ago, when she'd gotten pregnant with Tamela, Matthew hadn't welcomed the news. Their curly-headed moppet had been quite a surprise, just like *this* child would be.

She and Matthew hadn't planned to have children for at least another two years and, looking back, Rachel believed that Matthew probably hadn't wanted to extend their family at all. *She'd* been the one who'd fantasized about baby cribs and rattles. Matthew had been too busy with work and his father's incapacitation.

She could still see the old Matthew, dressed in a business suit with his tie askew, running both hands through his dark hair when she told him about her pregnancy.

"Didn't we decide to put off the babies?" he'd asked.

Rachel had rubbed a palm over her stomach, already in love with the thought of her child. She'd felt alienated because of Matthew's questioning tone. "I'll raise the baby on my own if I have to. Don't worry about it."

It'd been the wrong response. Matthew had cursed under his breath, then said, "This is just not a good time, Rachel. Dad's on his last legs and—"

"When *is* a good time?" she'd asked. She'd wanted to spike hurtful comments at him: *You'd rather baby your business* or *You'd rather nurse a whiskey bottle.*

But she'd kept her tongue, kept her silence. She'd been raised to keep the pain inside, so why change now?

Luckily, after Tamela's birth, Matthew had changed his tune, loving his daughter as much as he could. The baby had taken up his extra time. Time he used to spend with Rachel.

But she'd accepted the consequences, thinking that Tamela was lucky to have such an attentive father, thinking that she deserved the loneliness for getting pregnant in the first place.

She resumed her pacing. Would the new Matt feel the same way about this son or daughter? And what if he didn't want the child?

Rachel stopped in front of the mirror, not liking what she saw. The reflection featured a woman with faded gray-green eyes, her hair withered around her face. A woman whose smile had been chased away by too much worrying.

Before she told Matt about the pregnancy, she'd see Doc Perkins. After all, the home test could've been inaccurate.

She just wasn't sure what to hope for.

Rachel had been withdrawn this last week. Paler than usual. Matt was, by now, used to the healthy glow of her sun-warmed skin but, with the circumstances of his return to Kane's Crossing, she'd grown more wan everyday.

And it was because of him.

With that in mind, Matt piled his wife and daughter into the Cadillac and drove them to the Cutter's Lake shopping arcade.

The arched-ceiling, lakeside structure—a collection of small, quirky businesses all housed on a turn-of-the-century themed pier—had been Nick Cassidy's brainchild. An ice-cream parlor, lollipop store, vintage clothing boutique and antique emporium, among other ventures, all competed with the calliope-tinged energy of a merry-go-round and an amusement center.

It was a perfect place for families, and Matt thought it might cheer up his own wife and daughter.

Right now, they were strolling through the flower-dappled lane of shops on the way to the carousel. Tamela skipped several steps in front of them in her excitement.

Matt glanced at Rachel, thinking how *yee-haw* he must seem standing next to such a polished woman. She was wearing a linen skirt with another one of her vests, her hair in one of those fancy braids.

He said, "I haven't seen you smile since we got kicked out of the wedding reception."

She nodded, her full lips tightening. Then she said, "I've just been concerned with the farm and all."

"Dolly Llama is doing fine, Rache. She'll foal, and before you know it, Tarkin will be out of the picture."

"How can you be so sure?" She stopped walking, arms crossed over her chest.

Was it his imagination or was she more uptight than usual?

"I know." Matt rested his hands on his hips, inspecting the ground. "We could sure use that two hundred thousand dollars about now."

He looked up to see the carousel's colors and mirrored lights flashing behind her. Calliope music flirted around them, mocking their conversation.

He jerked his head toward the painted horses.

"Let's join Tamela. She's been bugging me about the merry-go-round for days."

Rachel's smile seemed forced. "I'm warning you. She's obsessed with it."

They bought tickets for Tamela and Matt. Rachel said she merely wanted to watch them from the gate.

Tamela selected a pink horse with a white mane. "This is Candy Cane, Daddy. I named her myself."

"She's good enough for the Derby," he said, helping his daughter mount the gaudy filly.

He strapped her in and, as the ride began to circle, kept a hand on Tamela's back to balance her. Every time they passed Rachel, the little girl waved. Rachel wiggled her fingers in return, evidently never tiring of the game.

When the ride finished, Matt blinked his eyes and decided never to brave the hellish contraption again. He didn't remember ever being so dizzy.

Not that he'd let Rachel know. Being whipped by poufy horses and loud circus music wasn't exactly the image he wanted to project.

Rachel turned away as they approached, one hand hiding something in front of her, one hand skimming her face. Matt wondered if she'd been crying again.

But why? What had he done now?

Tamela scampered up to Rachel, the girl's bunny-printed jumper flaring with her movements. "Did you see me, Mommy?"

She turned back to her daughter, composed and cool.

One hand was still hidden behind her back. "Oh, yes. You looked just like a princess."

Tamela hopped behind her mother, seizing her hand. Matt heard her yell, "Yay! Thank you!"

As the girl emerged with a glitter-laden princess hat, Rachel shrugged at Matt. Gesturing toward a hat cart, she said, "I couldn't resist buying it while you were disembarking from the ride."

Matt grinned. "Didn't they have any knight-in-shining-armor gear?"

"For you?" Rachel asked. "I was thinking more of a court jester costume."

Matt ground out a fake laugh. "You hear that, Tam? Mommy's feeling feisty today."

Finally. He was glad to see it.

Their daughter had already plopped the hat on her head. It was cone-shaped, with filmy pink material trailing from the top. "May I visit Esmerelda now?"

Rachel said yes, took her hand and started walking outside to the pier. Matt followed, adjusting his Stetson as the summer sun filtered over them.

Turned out that Esmerelda was one of those mannequins in a glass-paneled box, swathed in tacky scarves and a Gypsy blouse. Her frozen fingers hovered over a misty crystal ball. Painted above her head were the words "Your future is in my hands."

Lord help them.

Matt gave Tamela a quarter, and she slipped it into the machine with a decisive *clank*. Esmerelda waved her palms over the ball, stiff-featured. A piece of paper flew out of the slot.

Tamela chased it down and handed it to Rachel, who read it out loud.

"You will wield the sword of truth in your pursuit of justice." Rachel handed it back to her daughter. "I'm not sure princesses fight with pointy weapons."

Tamela peered around and ran over to a stick lying by a closed hot dog stand. "I can play with swords," she said, proceeding to swish the wood through the air.

Matt nodded, impressed. "Good wrist, Tam."

"Don't encourage her," said Rachel, hands on hips. "You be careful, young lady."

Tamela continued her newfound passion, jabbing at phantom opponents.

Matt sat on a nearby wrought-iron bench, kicking a boot over his other knee. He enjoyed his daughter's spirit, but he wanted to keep his eye on her, to see that she didn't bother passersby or talk to strangers.

After all, strangers were dangerous. But wasn't he—a virtual stranger—just as threatening to his family?

Rachel came into his view as she sat beside Matt, her attention locked on him. He could still see Tamela playing behind his wife.

"Have I told you that you get along really well with Tam?" asked Rachel.

"No need to mention it. She's my daughter."

Rachel bit her lip, her gaze dropping to the pier.

As he watched her, water lapped against wood, marking the passage of the awkward silence.

She sighed heavily. "Now is a good time to tell you, I guess. When I became pregnant with Tamela, you weren't exactly jumping for joy."

Her comment hit his gut with the force of an iron fist. The old Matthew hadn't wanted his daughter? This was too much to believe.

Matt shook his head, chuffing. "What a jerk."

Rachel's eyes widened a little. "Yeah, you were."

Damn, that was blunt. "I'm not the old Matthew," he said, fists bunching with caged anger.

He stood, unable to sit still, to take her distrust any longer. Good God, if he were his brother, Rick, maybe he'd understand Rachel's unwillingness to put her faith in him. His brother was dark, as rough as flint scratching against a match; he didn't exactly invite the warm fuzzies.

Matt wanted to think he was slightly different. Not that he was all puppy dogs and lollipops himself. But since he'd come back, what had he done that would make Rachel hate him so much?

The whole situation made him want to hit something. There was nothing he could do to change her attitude. Nothing at all.

But again, maybe the old Matthew was watching out for him. If Matt and Rachel had it easy, he might find himself falling for her again.

And that was out of the question.

He watched Tamela in her swordplay, wondering

how long he could remain a step removed from his family.

Rachel cleared her throat, bringing him back to the moment.

"Matt, I'm just curious." She took a deep breath, exhaled. "How would you, as you are now, have reacted when finding out that I was pregnant with Tamela? Even if it was unexpected?"

Matt knew she needed to hear his answer for peace of mind, and he couldn't blame her. However, he couldn't sugarcoat his answer; he couldn't lie to her. "I don't know what was going on in Matthew's life, Rache. I can't answer that fairly."

Her face fell, and it burned his heart. How could he have said something so stupid, so callous?

Once again, he'd blown it. But this time he took full responsibility. Her lowered gaze and trembling lip weren't Matthew's fault.

"I'm sorry," he said softly.

She shook her head, standing. A swift breeze caught her hair, flinging a strand over her eyes, masking the hurt he knew existed there.

"I'm sorry, too," she said.

Then she walked away, leaving him with more proverbial blood on his hands.

The next day, while collecting the garbage to take to the dump, he found a used pregnancy kit hidden at the bottom of a wastebasket.

At first he didn't get it. Then realization slammed into him.

Duh. This was Rachel's. They hadn't used protection in the garden house that night.

At first, a swell of pride and happiness flooded him. They were having a baby.

Then reality—and the fear caused by his tenuous situation—kicked in.

What dismal timing. Matt plucked out every available four-letter word from his vocabulary and barked it out, taking great satisfaction from the bathroom-tile echo. Tamela was at her summer school class, so there was no danger of her hearing the extent of his frustration.

The last thing he and Rachel needed was more emotional misadventures. A baby. You couldn't get more emotional than that.

What would they do if Matt regained his memory, becoming the man who might have another family tucked away somewhere? Come to think of it, how many kids did Matthew Shane already have?

Matt slammed his fist against a cabinet. He didn't deserve a child, an innocent who would only suffer for all his wrongdoings.

And he knew that his inability to commit hurt Rachel. At Cutter's Lake yesterday, when she'd asked him about Tamela and whether he would've been happy about her surprise pregnancy, he'd given the wrong answer.

Damn him.

Rachel must've been scared witless by now, thinking she was alone in having this baby.

But wasn't she? Would he stick around long enough to raise another child? If he reverted back to his old self, where would that leave Rachel and the new baby?

Matt needed to find out what was going on, so he rushed through his chore, hoping Rachel would be in the mood to give him some answers.

He found her in the living room sitting at a rosewood table, cards spread in front of her in a game of solitaire.

"How was your day?" she asked as he took a seat opposite her.

"Interesting." He steadied his shaking hands by clenching them under the table. *Get to the point,* he thought. *There's no use beating around the bush.* "I found the home pregnancy test."

She froze, dropping the Queen of Diamonds onto the other cards. Then, shoulders slumping, she closed her eyes. "I was hoping you wouldn't find out. For now, at least."

His voice was deceptively casual. "What were you going to do? Wait until you were out to here?" He relaxed his hands and held them in front of his belly.

"I don't know." She opened her eyes and straightened in her chair, gathering the cards, shuffling them.

He dropped his hands, bristling at her cavalier attitude. "Dammit, Rachel, this isn't a game. Are you sure you're pregnant?"

"Yeah. I went to Doc Perkins, and he confirmed it with a blood test."

Those four-letter words rose in his throat, nauseating him. He tried to react the way his former self wouldn't have reacted. Calm, rational, supportive...

He couldn't do it.

What if he regained his memory, ushering in a man who didn't even want Tamela?

Terror shrouded him, cold and threatening. What if he couldn't be a fit father for this child?

Rachel started dealing cards to him. "Like I told you last time. I'm prepared to take on the responsibility of this child myself. So don't worry, okay, Matt?"

"I'm...not worried." He stared at the cards in front of him. "You expect me to play poker right now? You're kidding."

She tilted her head to the side, fanning the cards in her hand, adjusting them. "It calms me down, like knitting. And, believe me, neither of us wants Rachel Shane holding a long needle right now. The best thing you can do is humor me with a few minutes of five-card draw."

Matt shrugged. All right, he'd do it her way. "Consider yourself humored."

His hand was lousy, so he exchanged four cards. Rachel tossed in two.

Still awful. Was this some cosmic comment on the hand life had dealt him? It was too ironic to consider.

He cocked his brow and prepared to bluff, his mind hardly on winning.

Rachel threw down the cards, and they scattered to the floor. "Dammit, Matthew. You're the worst card player. That eyebrow shoots up, and I know you're going to bluff."

Down went his cards. "Would you just talk to me?"

Her gray-green eyes flared like a patch of twilight sky. "What's to talk about?"

An off-color word escaped his lips. "I need you to be straight with me. What was it about our marriage that makes you so angry, Rachel? Tell me."

"You don't want to know."

"Tell me."

She stood, the force of her rage knocking back her chair. Her body trembled, carrying over to her voice. "I think you were having an affair, Matthew. How's that for the truth?"

For a second, Matt couldn't breathe. He could only think about green-blue nighties and that picture featuring a platinum-blond woman with her son.

Or maybe he could be more specific now.

His son.

Chapter Twelve

Rachel's stomach quivered with anger, her limbs quaking with the aftershock of her words.

She hadn't meant to tell him.

Matt looked as if the world had dropped out from under his feet. His whiskey-fume eyes had gone dark, and his mouth parted with apparent shock. "Why do you think I was having an affair?"

Her instinct formed the words "Never mind" on her lips, but she stopped herself. She'd been holding back the truth for years, and she was at her limit. Lying to Matt—to herself—hadn't made her life any easier; it'd merely shoved the pain into a tiny corner of her heart, where it'd grown year by year, swallowing all opportunities for happiness.

She crossed her arms over her chest, angling her chin, willing herself to keep a hold of her emotions. "Why did I suspect an affair? Maybe it was all those late hours you spent at the office. Maybe it was the way you'd smile at other women from across the room. Or maybe I devised such a wild idea because of the way you stopped treating me like a wife."

"Did I—did we…" Matt seemed stuck on the sentence.

Rachel took a deep breath, arming herself with that cool shield she used for protection. "Sure, we still slept together, but that's about it. Some part of me thought sex would keep us together. But that's not what the Captain and Tennille sang about, was it?"

"Love Will Keep Us Together." She tried to smile at her own joke, but it fell as flat as a slap-reddened open palm.

Matt didn't seem any more comfortable, his hat-tousled hair slumped over a furrowed brow.

Well, hell, why not tell him everything, since they were on the subject?

Rachel said, "You know, when we got married, I thought I wouldn't need to keep secrets anymore. I'd done enough of that for my mother."

Here Matt cocked his brow, and Rachel knew that she'd lost him. He didn't know anything about her mom.

But hadn't that been her goal?

She continued. "But once Tamela was born, you distanced yourself. I remember sitting home at eleven, twelve o'clock some nights, just waiting for you. Inevitably you'd have an excuse. 'Oh, Rachel, I needed to have a cocktail or two with the racing set. Gotta maintain those connections, you know.' Or 'Oh, Rachel, I needed to work on this-and-that account and I lost track of time.' "

Matt stood, and Rachel automatically took a step backward. Muted rage emanated from every hovering inch of him.

"I want to beat the stuffing out of Matthew," he said, teeth clenched. "But I can't."

Rachel shook her head. This wasn't right. Logic told her that she shouldn't punish this man standing before her. He hadn't committed Matthew's errors. Yet who else could she blame?

Herself.

God, she couldn't even admit it. Blaming herself would mean taking responsibility for Matthew's disappearance, for the lopsided state of their marriage. Her husband had been gone for over two years; he'd been a good scapegoat for all her worries and problems. She wasn't sure she was ready to let go of her bitterness.

She glanced at Matt, her heart twisting at the wounded concern in his gaze.

He pulled his mouth into a stark line. Then he asked, "Did you check up on me? To see if I was lying about my activities?"

"Yes." She could feel the guilt waiting, a midnight visitor watching her, judging her.

"And?"

And what, Rachel? she asked herself. *Tell him what you found out.*

She lost her composure, the guilt melting into her, its finger trailing a tear down her cheek. "I never found out anything concrete. But I could never shake the feeling that you didn't want to be with me anymore."

"Damn, Rache, how does that translate into an affair?"

The rough edges of his voice revealed his disgust. And she felt the same way about herself.

"Okay," she said, "maybe I was wrong. Maybe I just needed an excuse to explain your behavior."

"Or maybe you're just vilifying Matthew."

When Rachel shot a glare at Matt, all she saw was a tear-blurred shape. "What are you? The defense attorney?"

She heard another ground-out curse, vaguely saw him turn his back on her before the next hot tears spilled, clearing her vision.

So she might've been wrong about the affair, but she'd always felt a certain chill in her bones whenever Matthew hadn't come home. She'd always suspected the worst.

Maybe that made her a bad wife. But didn't that, then, deem her a perfect match for Matthew?

By now, Matt had faced her again, his hands resting on his hips, his face devoid of expression. Only the eyes—as brown as the charred edges of a love letter—held any emotion.

"Anything else you have to tell me?" he asked.

The last thing Rachel wanted was to make Matt hate her. And, judging by his cold posture, she'd done a pretty good job of that.

"I'm sorry, Matt." She wiped the moisture from her face with too much force, scratching a nail near her eye. The burn felt like a deserved penance. "My emotions got the better of me. It won't happen again."

His voice was barely above a whisper, scratchy and low. "You might as well air out that anger."

Bottled frustration stirred within her again. "Don't expect it. All right? Because whenever I get all touchy-feely like this I say too much. Just like my suspicions about the affair. I obviously overreacted."

Matt flinched, his shoulder slightly bucking backward. "How can you be sure?"

She could almost feel his doubt, the load of unsaid words barricaded by his simple statement. "I guess we can't be certain."

Tension wavered around them, between them, slanting at different angles like shafts of light. A shadow from a passing cloud filtered through the window and over Matt's eyes.

She thought of how Matthew had reacted to the news of Tamela's birth, and how he'd ultimately left them for over two years without a word of his safety.

The baby she was going to have shouldn't suffer

for her inability to keep Matthew's love. The baby should have a father who loved him or her, someone who could make a commitment to their family.

It was all too much. Rachel walked toward Matt, closing the distance. "Are you going to raise this child?"

He clenched his hands into fists. "You know I can't promise that, Rachel. I can't speak for Matthew, if he comes back."

"Damn you."

She pushed his broad chest, barely moving him.

He didn't react.

"Did you hear me?" she asked in a sob-choked voice. "Damn you."

She shoved him again, and he stood there, taking her pain.

His lack of response unnerved her. Suddenly she found herself punching his shoulders, tears streaming down her face, more than two years of self-doubt and pressure coming to the surface. It was as if another person had taken over her body and she was on the outside, watching this demented woman vent her anger.

After holding his ground for a few minutes, Matt finally shackled her flailing wrists with his hands, gripping them loosely. "Hey, you're hurting yourself."

Spent, Rachel leaned against his chest, her knees buckling. She wanted to tell him how sorry she was for losing control, but she couldn't.

They sank to the carpet, resting against a wall.

She didn't know what to expect of him. Would he gather his belongings and leave now? She wouldn't blame him if he did. She deserved it for her lack of poise.

Instead, he stroked her hair, resting his chin against her head, gentling her.

A jagged breath caught in her throat, one of those post-crying readjustments. "It's your turn to yell at me."

She could feel the slight smile of his lips against her scalp.

"That's the last thing our baby needs."

A hopeful surge of adrenaline flooded her limbs. As he brushed his fingers through her hair, holding her, Rachel relaxed, exhausted.

Before she shut her burning eyes, she took a chance.

"I hope you never get your memories back," she said, wondering if this was just another lie on her part.

Matt shifted, resting his cheek on her head, and Rachel thought, *Maybe we can get through this. Just maybe.*

An hour later, they were still sitting on the floor.

Rachel had drifted off to sleep, giving Matt time to recover from their latest confrontation.

Part of him had felt a glow of relief when she'd said that she hoped he wouldn't regain his memory.

Another part probably the place in his soul where Matthew still lived—had frozen.

What were they going to do if his memory returned? Would she hate the old Matthew for intruding?

This was ridiculous. That would mean hating him—the man he was right now—also. None of it made sense.

When he covered her stomach with his hand, Matt felt more torn than ever. What kind of future did this child have with half a dad? It wasn't fair to him or her.

But what if he could forget about his past mistakes, redeem himself, pledge his love to this child? Wasn't that possible?

Rachel stirred, lifting her head from his chest. Matt just wanted to lay her back down, to snap this moment into isolation and preserve its peace.

He ran his knuckles down her soft cheek, noticing the slightly swollen scratch she'd given herself while wiping away tears.

She sighed and rubbed her face against his shirt. "This is nice."

Good Lord, he hoped she wasn't getting too attached to him. Even if the idiot-soft side of him kind of liked the thought of having a baby with Rachel, Matt knew it still wasn't a good idea. That particular side had wanted to belong to someone, had brought him back to the horse farm, had gotten him into this mess in the first place.

He'd have to bury that part of himself before it found another streak of trouble.

They leaned against each other for a moment, breath echoing breath.

Then Rachel spoke. "I don't want you to think that we never had good times."

He thought about the scattered pieces of his Seville memories. "I know."

She sketched her fingertips along his ribs, along his dully throbbing scar. "One of my favorite memories is when we made love in the abandoned barn over the hill. Afterward we went to the creek that runs through our property and bathed each other."

Heat shot through his body. He could imagine laying his hands on Rachel, splashing water over her skin until the moisture beaded itself over her goose bumps. "You're taunting me."

She peered up at him, gray-green irises swept over by dark lashes. "I didn't mean to. We have other good memories I can tell you about."

Matt wished he could create wonderful times for her, too. He wished he were free enough to strengthen their marriage for the sake of Tamela and the new baby. But, in his heart, he wasn't sure if he could live up to any promises he made. "Be my guest. I can use as many memories as I can get."

Settling farther against him, Rachel seemed content. "Let's see. There was the way you proposed to me in Madrid. It was during a military parade, and you just turned to me and belted out, 'Marry me, Rachel!'" She laughed. "I thought we were going to be questioned by the authorities. They gave us scary glares."

Matt grinned. "That was a pretty brave move during a show of force."

"We lived." Rachel paused. "Then there was Tamela's first birthday, when you bought her a doll she wouldn't be able to play with until much later. It was sweet, and you didn't know any better, but that didn't stop her from smiling for hours at you."

Familiarity bunched like a flexed fist inside Matt. It was as if his mind was trying to grasp the feelings and images. "I suppose I would've been more knowledgeable if I'd increased my time with Tamela."

"She was too young to remember much. That's why she's far more forgiving than I am."

Thank goodness one of them was vigilant about getting too close to the other. "Being cautious is a natural reaction to what I put you through."

Once again, Rachel's words punched through his thoughts. *I think you were having an affair.*

Even if she wasn't so sure, Matt had a bad feeling he was. How else could he explain those images he'd been having?

Rachel had softened against him, one arm draped over his thigh, her other arm curled between his ribs and biceps, her head still resting against his chest.

Matt wondered if this afternoon's emotional meltdown had allowed her the freedom to relax her guard. He wondered if she had let go of her frustration.

The thought didn't give him any comfort.

"Cautious?" she asked. "I've always been cautious."

He remembered what she'd said about her mother. "Are you talking about your dear old mom?"

A long hesitation made him think she wasn't going to answer. But she surprised him.

"Yeah. My mother. God, I love her so much, but at the same time…"

Matt waited while Rachel gathered her words.

She scratched a fingernail up and down his shirt.

"I was ten years old the first time I saw my mom with another man. I'd ditched prep school that day, not that I did it often. I had some kind of test I knew I was going to bomb, so I just didn't face it. My dad was going to be disappointed either way, so I thought avoiding the prolonged exam discomfort was the best option. I couldn't stand the thought of him saying, 'Rachel, I thought you could do better. This hurts me.' Because his pain hurt me, too. It was worse than a spanking or any other punishment.

"Anyway, I decided to watch soap operas all day, then double back and pretend like I was coming home from school. I didn't even make it to my room when I heard noises from down the hall. No one was supposed to be home during the day, so I was afraid.

"I got one of my dad's golf clubs from the closet and crept to my parents' door, and..."

She caught her breath. Matt could feel her heart jackhammering against his arm.

"There she was, on top of some guy. No clothes. It was such an awful sight, so I ran and ran. I didn't come back until after dinner.

"She caught me before I made it through the door. She must've been watching through the window for me. I didn't get into trouble for ditching school. In fact, my mom was very accommodating, promising me new clothes and a new TV. She didn't have to tell me why, but I asked anyway. She took my elbow and dragged me into my room, shutting the door.

"She said, 'I know what you saw, Rachel. Now, you know Dad has a weak heart. If you tell him about me, he'll probably have a heart attack and die. Do you want to be responsible for that?'"

"Jeez," said Matt, tightening his fingers in Rachel's hair.

Rachel nodded. "Nice, huh? But every time I thought of telling him, I'd imagine him doubling over in pain, leaving me and Mom by ourselves. I didn't want that.

"Then, life got stranger and stranger. Mom would start picking fights with Dad, probably because she wanted some punishment for what she was doing to him. To us." Rachel hesitated. "Dad would only raise his voice, then forget about Mom's accusations. He's the most forgiving man on earth, but I thought he'd never forgive my mother's affairs.

"In spite of his big heart, I kept my mouth shut every day, even when my mom would sneak through my window late at night. I knew what she was doing but, at the same time, she knew I'd never tell. I didn't want to break my family apart, so I kept my silence. As a matter of fact, you're the first person I've told."

Matt was taken aback. "You didn't even tell me before the amnesia?"

"No. I was too mortified. I didn't want to air my misfortunes and taint our lives. I didn't even mention my suspicions about your supposed affairs."

Now he could understand the reason Rachel hadn't wanted to talk about their strained marriage. She'd just wanted to keep her family together, just like she'd done with her own parents.

Matt tilted her chin with a forefinger until she faced him. Her cheeks flushed a soft red color, bringing life to her gaze.

"You need to talk with your parents," he said.

She shut her eyes, averted her face. "It doesn't matter now. What good would it do?"

"Doesn't your father deserve to know?"

Silence. Then, "I love both my parents very much. Nobody has the perfect family, Matt."

He tried to avoid the niggling little voice inside him that said, "You just might have *two* imperfect families, Mattie. How's that for keeping up with the Joneses?''

He mentally brushed off the reminder, hating the fact that he'd been angry with Rachel for doing the exact same thing: avoiding problems by not facing them.

Instead, he said, ''Rachel, you're not going to find that peace you've been hoping for unless you take care of this.''

''I hate when you're right.'' She pulled away from him, keeping her arm on his thigh.

The extended contact tightened his body, making him ache for more. ''Get used to it.''

He hadn't meant the words as a promise, but her gaze told him that's what she'd heard.

In fact, he didn't like what he saw in her eyes.

Tenderness, a wary acceptance. A softness only a few heartbeats away from love.

No, he had to be mistaken. Love wasn't in their plans. *Couldn't* be in their plans.

He stood abruptly, distancing himself from Rachel. ''It's about time to pick up Tamela. I'll take care of her.''

''But I—''

''No,'' he interrupted, hating his gruff response, hating the way she bit her lip.

''No,'' he said less forcefully. ''You take a break.''

He left, never looking back as he went about his business.

And later that night, as he twisted the bedsheets around his body in a mockery of sleep, he bolted up in bed.

Sudden memories, ones he wanted to erase.

Memories he'd seen through the haze of liquor. Images of half-dressed women, draped over bourbon-shaded chairs. Pictures of a whisker-dark face staring back at him through a dingy, one-star hotel mirror.

Rachel's confessions had triggered more flashbacks, and Matt didn't like what he was seeing.

Matthew was getting closer.

Chapter Thirteen

Rachel couldn't help herself. She was falling back in love with her husband.

Or maybe she'd just plain fallen in love with a new man altogether.

Three days ago they'd had the fight to end all fights. She'd pushed him, thrown insults at him and, still, he'd remained strong and tender. At that point, she'd come to the conclusion that Matt was his own man, that she'd been wrong to charge him with Matthew's mistakes.

She also knew she had some repenting of her own to do, not the least of which was to decide whether or not to tell her father about her mother's affairs.

Well, she wouldn't ruin her good mood right now

with something that had dogged her for years. She'd have to think about her parents later.

At the moment she wanted to deal with Matt.

Rachel sat down on the blanket she'd spread over a tuft of hay. She breathed in the sweet, pungent scent of old barn, watching as the afternoon light vented through the slats of grayed wood, the illumination giving freedom to the dust motes riding the air.

She'd sent a note to Matt, requesting his presence in the abandoned structure. And it was wicked, really, to do so. When she'd told him about one of her favorite memories—making love in this barn—his arms had tightened around her, his heart had thumped double time through her own skin.

No matter how he kept that three-step distance or remained stoically removed as she hurled accusations, Rachel knew he wanted her.

And she felt the same way.

She'd realized something while lying in his arms after the fight: Matt was looking after her in his own quiet way. That thought had wrapped a cocoon of safety around her heart, warming her blood with the strength of Matt's sinewy arms.

Rachel smiled and spread a hand over her stomach. It was still flat, giving no indication of her pregnancy, but she could almost feel the baby forming inside her. Maybe Matt could learn to love the both of them.

Footsteps sounded outside, and she knew it was her husband.

Rachel sat on the blanket, tucking her dress around

her ankles, resting her hand over the old-fashioned wicker picnic basket.

A shadow pulled itself over the ground, stretching in the sunlight like a dark ray.

"Knock, knock," said a deep voice.

Rachel suppressed a quiver of longing. "Come in."

The shadow clenched, ebbing back into the all-too-human form of her husband. He'd shoved his hands into his jeans' pockets, leaning against the rickety entrance. "You summoned?"

She smiled at his teasing tone. Ever since their emotional blowout, they'd been on friendly terms, easy and slow with their jokes and smiles.

Patting the blanket, Rachel beckoned to him. "I thought you could use a break from all the employees' snickers."

She knew that the other men thought Matt was touched in the head for wearing his Western duds. Kentucky-bluegrass horse handlers wore breeches and jodhpurs complemented by sleek riding boots; they didn't kick around in Wranglers and dusty Justins.

Matt sauntered inside the barn, flutters of loose hay and dust winking around his ranch-honed body. "Ask me if I care about fashion sense," he said.

A primal urge stroked her from the inside out. *Just relax,* she told herself. *You're just being civil, eating lunch with your hard-working husband.*

"Stop with the smooth tone, cowboy." And she

meant it. Really. "I fixed a little lunch for you. Otherwise you wouldn't bother to eat."

Matt stood in front of her, his height forcing Rachel to crane her neck. Then he lowered himself to the blanket, his mouth straightening, devoid of laugh lines.

"Peter Tarkin was here."

The name imploded her good mood. "What, did Dracula come to suck the blood out of us?"

Matt grinned slightly. "He tried, but we've reached an understanding. Tarkin likes your plan for Dolly Llama's foal. He thinks it'll bring in a lot of money."

Rachel plopped to her back, arms outstretched. "I've already told him that, the moth-eaten coot."

"I hate to say it, Rache, but Tarkin is old school. He doesn't think much of a woman running his business."

That maddening half smile lit over Matt's mouth. Rachel either wanted to slap it off or kiss it.

"So," she said, "are you telling me that he's content, now that you're helping with the farm?"

"Content?" Matt chuckled. "Far from it. The pressure's still on. If we don't deliver on our promises next year, he *will* be hounding us again. No doubts there."

Summer sweat dampened her chest, and Rachel fanned herself in time to the songs outside the barn: the endless sigh of windswept grass, the low hum of hidden insects. The hot season made her feel lazy. Slightly sinuous.

She peeked out of the corner of her eye at Matt and, sure enough, he was running a slow gaze over her body.

On his way back up, he caught her look, frowning. "We've had some peaceful days lately."

Why was he suddenly so serious? She'd gotten several heavy thoughts off her chest, had told him about Matthew's suspected affairs and her mother-induced guilt. Rachel couldn't help feeling a little giddy at his acceptance of her imperfections.

There was a lot to be relieved about.

"Yeah, I suppose we've become regular buddies," she said, rolling her eyes.

"What's with the spin-cycle gesture?"

"Nothing."

Matt chuffed. "I suppose that's female speak for 'You're in a world of trouble, pal.'"

"No, really. Nothing is wrong. Everything is peachy keen. In fact, I love having a husband who's got the libido of an android."

He glanced away. "Rachel, you know you're into some dangerous territory."

She pursed her lips, barring words. Not that she was going to say something hurtful—she'd had her fill of that these past few weeks—but she didn't want to beg her own husband to touch her.

Heck, maybe it wasn't such a great idea anyway. Especially when they seemed to have come to a truce.

Once again, that sneaky word *love* crept into her mind.

Go away, she thought.

"That's okay." She sighed, rising to her elbow to flip open the picnic basket. "You don't ever have to touch me again."

Just as Rachel was reaching for some grapes, Matt caught her wrist. The light pressure sent her heart flipping through her chest.

"Remember what happened the last time we were together?" he asked. "We made a baby."

Rachel glared at his circled fingers, then at him. "Surely someone taught you the birds and bees on that Texas ranch. I'm already pregnant. It can't happen again until about eight months from now."

"Are you issuing an invitation?"

"You've got to be kidding. We don't need any more trouble in our lives. I'm comfortable with the status quo."

Liar.

To prove her point, she leaned back on the blanket with what she hoped was a careless grin on her lips.

His body shadowed her. Minutes passed as they locked stubborn gazes. When he finally spoke, the timbre of his voice sent a fizz of electricity straight through her body.

"You can't stand the thought of me leaving you here high and dry." He grinned.

The expression ticked her off. "You know, I'd rather be romanced by the Siggy Woods Monster."

"No such thing as monsters."

She angled her head, positioning her mouth right beneath his. Ha. Let him stay sane now.

"I beg to differ, Matt Shane. Don't you remember anything about Kane's Crossing legends?"

He bent closer to her, their lips a breath apart. "Enlighten me."

"You really don't remember."

Of course Matt didn't recall any tales from his old life in Kane's Crossing. He only remembered pointless details that rode the edges of his own nightmares.

No, he thought. Don't sink into your black pit of a life again. Think about your wife. Think about her body stretched beneath yours. Think about your child waiting to be born.

He softened his voice. "You're baiting me."

Rachel uttered a little "hmph." Then, "If you must know, the Siggy Woods Monster dwells in…where else…the woods. Your sister lives on the fringes of them."

"Lacey? Doesn't it scare a woman who lives by herself?"

Rachel tilted her head back the slightest degree, inviting his kiss. When he ignored her body language, she sighed, shifting beneath him, making him stiff with need.

She warmed his lips with her soft breath. "Lacey doesn't act kindly to sympathy, Matt. She's as stubborn as the day is long. Sound familiar?"

Rachel rubbed against him, and Matt groaned.

She said, "Is that a stallion in your pocket, or are you just ready to ride?"

Matt backed away, but not by much. Even with his better judgment screaming in his ear, he couldn't keep his hands off her. He ran a fingertip over her collarbone, tracing the shivering circles of sunlight on her skin. Rachel stretched her arms over her head, clearly enjoying the attention.

Damn, he hated himself for giving in. But wasn't this far better than fighting with Rachel?

He said, "I thought we weren't going to sleep together anymore."

"That was before..." Rachel flushed. "Yeah, that's what I said, all right."

For a tense minute, Matt thought she was going to murmur something deadly. Something about love, an emotion neither of them could afford with Matthew hanging over their heads.

His instinct confirmed his fears. Rachel had the soft-eyed look of a woman in love. It was a one-hundred-and-eighty-degree turn from the morning he'd returned to the horse farm.

Matt's jaw tightened. "Don't think that a few good days between us is going to change anything, Rachel."

She reached out to wind a strand of his hair around her finger. Dammit, even a tiny touch could arouse him.

She said, "A few good days can pile up into an understanding. If we agree to take our relationship one day at a time, maybe we can avoid disappointment."

"He's coming back, you know."

The words popped out of his mouth before he could stop them. But they were true. They'd merely needed a voice.

Rachel eased off his hat and slid all of her fingers into his hair, massaging his scalp, just like she'd done weeks ago, when he'd first returned.

"But what if you don't regain those memories, Matt? What if we could start over, almost like two people who just met?"

Her desperate naiveté touched him. "Because we have a lot of baggage, Rache. We can't ditch the past."

She lowered her hands, letting them flop to her sides. Her mouth pulled down at the edges, and he wanted to tip the corners back into a smile with a few well-placed kisses.

"The other day," she said, "I realized that hanging on to the past isn't doing any good. You helped me to see that, Matt. Why can't you do the same thing?"

Yeah. Why?

"We can't pretend that Matthew never existed. It won't work." *Because he's coming back.*

Couldn't she understand that?

She said, "You're so natural with Tamela. And with the business—"

"Are you trying to convince me to fend off the memories?" His laugh was low and unconvincing.

"I've told you that Matthew and I aren't the same person, but I was wrong. We share everything—body, soul…"

"Wife, children," she added, her eyes glossy with oncoming tears.

Without thinking, Matt reached over and brushed his fingertips over her stomach.

Rachel cupped his face in her hands, her skin a balm against his heat. "We can work together, Matt. We can overcome the problems we had in our marriage. In fact, maybe this has all been a blessing in disguise. Maybe we can start over."

Dammit, she was talking him into something he couldn't handle right now. How could he make decisions for Matthew?

As if she'd read his mind, Rachel continued. "What if you never remember, Matt? Five, ten years from now, will you still refuse to move on because the old Matthew hasn't come back yet?"

She'd said the right words, had hit on the logic he needed to hear. It'd been over two years since he'd lost his memory in the New Orleans streets. How long would he put off his life until he got back the missing pieces?

Matt leaned over, nuzzling Rachel's neck, feeling the hum of her veins through his lips. "I don't want to hurt you and the kids. I don't want to mess up your lives again."

"You won't," she said, her words vibrating under Matt's mouth. "I'll make sure you can't wound us."

His scar began pulsing, just as it did every time he came too near his wife. It beat between his ribs with the echo of a lone drum—hollow and tuneless. With every empty note, Matt came closer to the realization that he was lacking something vital inside his soul.

He was missing a family. Missing Rachel.

She belonged to him, within him, and he didn't have the strength to fight her anymore.

Matt glided his hand from her collarbone to the buttons of her dress, undoing them deliberately, sliding the plastic discs through the holes with one hand. His blood thickened, weighing down his skin with heat.

She wasn't wearing a bra today. The outfit's spaghetti straps and backless dip didn't allow it. As he peeled open her top, Matt drew in a breath, his gaze going red at the sight of her breasts.

They'd swollen since the night in the garden house. He'd heard pregnancy did that to a woman.

And thank you, nature. The hardened tips of her breasts had flushed a deep pink, ripe as sin. When he cupped the underside of one, Rachel gasped, arching against him.

Matt lightened his touch, drawing on instinct once again. He hadn't been with a woman since his amnesia, hadn't wanted the possible strings attached. But this was different. This was his wife.

His wife.

He coaxed his knuckles around her nipple. "Tell

me another one of your favorite memories,'' he whispered.

Her voice was breathy. "Besides making love in this barn?''

"Right.''

She shut her eyes, lips parting as he continued exploring her skin. He fit the length of his fingers over her ribs, skimming the slick arches of bone.

"Um, my brain's not exactly working right now, Matt.'' She stroked the underside of his arm, her fingers tickling upward to a tender spot near his chest.

Something close to a sated growl rumbled in his throat. "Everything else—''

He bent to cover her lips with his, brushing his tongue inside her mouth, their kiss stealing endless moments from the lazy drawl of an early July.

He pulled away and finished his sentence. "—is in perfect order.''

Then he lowered his head again, this time to trace his tongue over her nipple, sucking it, laving it with a gentle rhythm. She held him closer as the hay crunched beneath the blanket, rustling with every move they made.

Sliding his hands up her slim thighs and under her dress, Matt worked her panties downward, trailing a thumb through the moist cleft between her legs as he went along.

One of Rachel's legs bucked slightly, and he couldn't help grinning. He glanced up. "Have you had enough time to think?''

He tossed her grandma drawers to the side and leaned on an elbow. With his free hand, he teased the soft skin of her inner thighs, feeling them get goose bumpy.

"Mmmm. Waterfalls. Driving all day on country roads. Staring at the sky and making plans with you... Please, Matt, don't stop."

The images had sounded so familiar, but they were gone before they could settle in to a concrete picture in his mind's eye.

Who cared now? Matt was used to the shortcomings of his brain.

He ignored his empty spaces, tracing his fingertips back up her leg, slipping inside Rachel's heat, slicking his fingers in and out to the song of her moans.

The baby. He didn't want to crush their child, didn't want to bring needless pain to him or her.

Matt withdrew and rolled onto his back, Rachel following his lead, climbing on top of him while unbuttoning his shirt with agonizing care.

Her dress wilted over her arms, almost like Spanish moss curving against the wind. The afternoon sun filtered through the thin material, silhouetting every movement. Her breasts peeked through the drape of cotton, and Matt couldn't stop his hands from palming their fullness.

He could feel the center of her pulsing over his arousal, heating him to distraction. As she parted his shirt and scratched over his chest with infinite patience, Matt didn't care about who he was anymore.

Now he was just a man. A man who'd been born to have this woman be a part of him.

She'd undone his jeans, easing inside, lightly grasping him, stroking him. He watched her through half-closed eyes, wishing she'd just slip him inside of her.

"See?" she whispered. "I was right. You *are* ready to ride, cowboy."

And when she shifted forward, ready to guide him in, Matt reached up, running a thumb near her eye. The hint of a scratch still burned with a pink glow, and Matt remembered how his heart had contracted when she'd wiped away those angry tears just days ago.

He didn't need to say a word. When her gaze connected with his, Rachel pressed her palm over his hand, leaning her cheek against him.

"I know," she said, angling her mouth against his skin, kissing his fingers. "I know."

She led him inside of her, moving her hips to accommodate him, closing her eyes and opening her mouth before biting a lip.

This felt so right, almost like Eve joining with Adam to replace that missing rib.

Heat suffused him, inching along his body, throb by throb. He was mindless, lost in the Kentucky humidity, swallowed by its swirl of sweat-pearled skin and slow sunsets. Even if this lovemaking was sapping the strength from him, he wanted more.

Damn, she fit him like a wedding ring.

He wasn't sure he could go back to being the civil farm hand who lived down the hall from Rachel's bedroom. He wanted to be in there every night, arching against her, listening to her breathe while the rest of the house hummed with silence. He wanted to taste her jasmine skin, to run his mouth over the curve of her calf.

He wanted more than he deserved.

As reality slammed into him, his mind blanked to a held of white static, bursting back into a fast-forward filmstrip of blurred images:

Painted faces he didn't know, rain-slicked streets that reflected neon red, the smell of bourbon and exotic spices, the fire of whiskey on his tongue.

Matt held Rachel tightly, spending himself, groaning with his climax.

Then he pleasured his wife until she writhed with her own flashes of ecstasy.

Afterward, as they lay on the blanket covering the hay, their breaths shallow pants racing to keep up with their echoing heartbeats, Matt closed his eyes to the pictures attacking his mind.

Pictures of that sheer nightie. Pictures of a woman marking his back with her nails.

Matthew Shane was a bastard, and Matt supposed he could be filed right under the same category.

Later, they'd cooled their bodies in the stream. Matt's belly had tightened as he'd watched Rachel, lying back in the water, the current streaming through her hair like clouds threading through ribbons. They'd held each other until the sky grew dark with the hint of a summer storm, until it came time to pick up Tamela from her school program.

All the while Matt had pushed back his guilt. Why had he allowed himself to make love with Rachel again? Every day he was getting deeper and deeper into this relationship. Deeper into trouble.

As he plopped down to his bed after a dinner during which he tried his best to avoid Rachel's loving gaze, he thought, *You're going to make your wife a cold woman again.*

And there was no one else to blame for his careless use of her.

Matt stared at the duffel bag on his floor, then ground a boot heel into it, cursing. What kind of a father was he anyway? The type who came home for occasional dinners and left a trinket of affection to apologize for the lack of time he spent with his family?

That's what he was becoming. And he'd be damned if he turned into Matthew Shane again.

He heard Rachel walk down the hall toward her own bedroom, already having tucked Tamela into bed. He wondered if she expected him to stay the night with her.

The duffel bag gaped open, unzipped, staring up at him with wide-eyed indifference. Denim and silver mingled inside of it, tempting Matt to try once again to touch the objects, to pull memories from their textures.

He grasped a comb, running a finger over the bristles, watching as it gleamed in the lamplight. Nothing. No memories.

Whipping out a belt buckle from the bag, Matt repeated the process of summoning information from his belongings. Again, his mind was a past-life blank.

He mulled over every possession, wishing he had the guts to enter Rachel's bedroom and hunt down Matthew's belongings, his clothes, his cuff links. Anything might've helped.

Ah, damn. He couldn't go near Rachel and her puppy-dog eyes, her hopeful smile. There was no way he could resist her again. Not after this afternoon. Not after the way he'd broken every promise he'd made to himself about keeping her safe from him.

Frustrated, Matt picked up the remote control and snapped on the television set. He perched on the mattress's edge, running a hand over his face.

Maybe the tube would clear his mind. He could zombie out in front of it without having to deal with his own problems. At least for a while.

He rested his forearms on his thighs, hunkering over with strained concentration, squinting at the TV.

A quiz show. Nope, watching people who had nothing to do but fill their minds with useless data irritated him right now, especially since so much information had escaped him.

He channel surfed for a moment, lighting on a

cops-and-robbers show. Yeah, okay, he could live with this. A little testosterone, a little justice.

His mind cleared itself as he fell into the lure of the airwaves. Red-and-blue warnings, bad men being chased and violent crime stories. Good television.

Matt leaned farther forward as some bit players reenacted a mugging. His heart pounded in his ears as he stared at the victim, lying on the ground with a halo of blood circling his head.

With a blinding flash of lightning, his scar screamed for attention in a burst of hot-white pain. Matt sucked in his breath, his mind whirling with colors and pictures as the television program's voice-over rose in volume like an approaching siren. He fumbled for the remote, shutting off the TV with a resounding click.

His breath chopped through his lungs, burning with the heat of his rib wound. Matt slid open his shirt and pressed a palm over the pain, trying to stifle it, but the searing agony just increased.

Just as suddenly, the pounding stopped, allowing Matt to collect himself. He waited, expecting the wound to act up again. Nothing.

Dammit, he'd been close to reliving something. What the hell had it been?

He ran a finger over his pale slash of a scar. Its sharpness reminded him of the crisp edge of a dollar bill. Two hundred thousand-dollar bills, to be exact.

Then it was there. The speck of a memory, as insignificant as a water spot on a glass, but just as noticeable.

He burst out of his room, ran down the hall and knocked on Rachel's door.

When she opened it, he barely registered the shy smile, the half-anxious gray-green shade of her gaze.

Then her face melted into a mask of realization, wan with doubts. Her nervous voice burbled past him, over his head.

"Oh, great. This must be where you tell me what a mistake we made this afternoon," she said, barely stopping for a breath. "I know, I know. You feel like you're being roped into this. You probably feel desperate to find closure with your life—"

"Rachel—"

"—and just move on without a problem like me—"

He squeezed her shoulders, forcing her to a pause. Had he hurt her, reached out too forcefully?

Gentling his touch, Matt looked into her eyes.

"I remember what happened to that two hundred thousand dollars."

Her mouth clamped shut.

Chapter Fourteen

A stunned silence followed Matt's pronouncement.

Rachel swallowed, feeling lightheaded. His body swayed in front of her in a sick, waltzing blur, but she knew he wasn't doing the dancing. It was her own brain.

"Just, out of the blue, you know where it is?" she asked.

Matt nodded, and she noticed that his shirt was partially opened, revealing the slash between his ribs.

Rachel's blood heated again while she remembered their afternoon activities. She glanced away, embarrassed to admit, even with body language, that she'd fallen as deeply in love with Matt as she had with the old Matthew.

He lowered his voice. "I was watching TV when something kicked on in my brain. I can't explain it. I—"

He stopped.

"What?" Rachel reached a hand out to him.

Grasping her fingers, Matt accepted her support. "I'm not sure of the details, but I think I went to New Orleans to pay off a gambling debt."

It felt as if someone had slammed her body against a wall. She couldn't breathe, couldn't focus, every nightmare she'd ever harbored about Matthew mocking her newfound trust in this man.

All she could do was back away from him, shaking her head.

She saw her husband clearly for the first time since his return. Even with the jeans and boots, he was still Matthew, disappointing her yet another time, making her wonder if keeping his shortcomings a secret from Tamela was worth the price of her well-being.

She couldn't go through it again. She'd grown out of the desperate need to keep secrets.

He must've seen the naked distrust in her eyes, because Matt's face had fallen. He reached out a hand to her. "Rachel, I don't know anything else. I wish I could explain why I did it."

"Explanations don't matter anymore." She clenched her fists. "Even Chloe Lister's information hasn't helped us get past our problems."

He folded his arms across his chest, covering the scar. "Chloe is still working for you?"

Rachel nodded. Not even his injured gaze could soften the damage of this latest news, and she wouldn't be fool enough to give him the benefit of the doubt again.

Matt cursed. "I can't believe it. You never trusted me. When we were making love, when you told me about your mother...all the while you couldn't put your faith in me. You didn't believe that I've changed."

"Have you?" Her words came with the speed of arrows. "I'm just as unhappy now as I was two years ago."

It was a lie. She'd thought that it would feel good saying it, that the words would protect her, but she was wrong. She regretted it, regretted the stunned look on his face.

"There it is," he said softly. "I don't think there's anything left to say."

He left Rachel standing in her room. She could hear his boots scuffing down the hallway carpet, could hear him shuffling around his room. A door shut, another one eased open.

Had she finally hurt him enough to drive him away?

Oh, God. Had she been trying to get rid of him all along? Wounding him before he could do the same to her?

She crossed her forearms over her belly. Matt was a part of her, a part of their children. He couldn't go.

With a burst of remorse, Rachel bolted down the

hall. His room was empty. Then, as she continued her search, she saw that Tamela's door was cracked open. She peeked inside.

Her husband kneeled at their daughter's bedside, smoothing back the sleeping child's curly hair. She heard him whispering to her.

"Hey, Tam. I can't bring myself to get you up. You're probably having great dreams, and I don't want to ruin them."

Rachel thought of Matt's first night home, and how he'd read Tamela a bedtime story. Even then, he'd shown an easy sense of love for their daughter. Rachel knew now that she just couldn't let him walk out the door, away from Tamela and their new child.

She'd apologize when he finished talking with Tamela.

He continued. "I'm sorry for coming back and messing things up. I did a great job of that, didn't I? But life turns out the way it does for good reasons. I don't pretend to know what's happening in this particular situation, but I'll respect God's plans."

Rachel held back a sob, hating herself for hurting him again. Hating that he was too much at odds with his old life to think himself worthy of the new one.

Matt must've sensed her presence, because he looked her way. Tiny raindrops tapped on the window, the reflection flecking his body with dark marks. Marks she'd held against him.

He turned his attention back to Tamela, and his cold dismissal stung Rachel.

"I'm not going to desert you or your brother or sister, Tam. I hope that promise works itself inside your smart little head." He paused. "Just remember that Daddy loves you."

He kissed Tamela's temple, pausing to watch her sleep. Moments later, he stood, fitting his hat over his brow, towing both his duffel bag and a stiff attitude toward Rachel.

He walked right past her, and she shut the door, following him down the hall, down the stairs, into the foyer.

"Matt?"

He slung the bag over a broad shoulder, watching her expectantly.

She couldn't believe that all he owned in this world could be contained in one bag. The thought made her want to cry.

He said, "If you're feeling sorry about what you said, don't bother. We can't keep playacting like this marriage is working."

"But it was working for a while," she said. "And I'm still going to apologize for my outburst. I didn't mean it."

"Rachel." He tipped up his hat. "You meant it. And you'll mean everything you say until you come to terms with Matthew. Until *I* come to terms with Matthew."

He was really going to leave. She thought of Tamela and how his leaving a second time would affect their daughter. "Don't go. Please don't leave us. The farm's doing better with you here, and—"

He'd chuffed when she mentioned the farm, and she felt embarrassed at herself for avoiding the real issues.

He said, "As I told Tamela, I won't desert anyone. But I can't stay here, Rache. We both know that. Living as husband and wife won't be the answer to our problems." His eyes took on a grim darkness. "Besides, the kids don't need a role model who doubles as a bad seed."

"Where are you going?" She couldn't believe he was serious, couldn't believe that she was almost desperate for him to stay.

"Tonight I think the Edgewater Motel will do. After that... Who knows? I need to think about what's going on, to work out these memories. Because they are coming back, Rachel, whether we want them to or not."

Rachel had never humiliated herself, had never begged with anyone or cried for attention. But she wanted to let go of her poise, to ask him for another chance.

Yet she couldn't do it. Pleading like a melodramatic fool went against her grain, no matter how much Matt had come to mean to her.

"All right, Matthew." She saw him flinch at the name. "You work things out. Take some time. Find yourself. Have a regular ball on your quest for manhood."

Once again, she immediately regretted the words because she hadn't meant any of them.

He paused, his gaze lowered. A bitter grin slashed over his lips. "I deserve your mistrust. Every minute of it. And that's why it's best for me to go."

"Wait." A moment of clarity slapped her. She cleared her throat of its tightness, despising the sad ache that came with her realization. "You're scared to death that I'll hate you when you get the memories back, aren't you? You're afraid to become the old Matthew."

He straightened, as if remembering something else. "Goodbye, Rachel."

He opened the door, letting in the sound of raindrops. The storm outside was gathering in anger and intensity.

As he walked out the door, tears trailed down Rachel's cheeks. She followed him, then leaned against the frame, collecting all the courage in her body.

"I love you," she said, her voice wobbling.

He turned around, glancing at her belly, his eyes softening with a guilty sheen. Then he said, "I really believe that you want to love me, Rachel."

She heard different words. Words spoken by her own conscience: *You still have too much anger to let me into your heart.*

She couldn't respond, unable to form the words to change his mind about leaving.

As she watched him saunter toward the garage, a lone figure in the midst of hovering darkness, Rachel thought of everything he was taking with him. Things that didn't fit into the duffel bag.

He was taking the smiles he'd shared with Tamela, taking every moment of happiness she'd felt since he'd returned.

He was taking her life to a run-down motel on the outskirts of Kane's Crossing, and she wouldn't be there with him to unpack.

She couldn't help thinking that she wouldn't ever be with him again.

The sky was a void of darkness, and Matt was driving right into it.

The trees lining the country road had a surreal quality, their branches looming in his headlights, tossing heavy droplets onto his windshield.

Matt thought of slowing down, but he couldn't. He wanted to get as far away from Rachel as possible.

No. Scratch that. He wanted to be with her. God, he really did. But he didn't want the reminder of Matthew's sins slapping his face everyday.

Just the pain in Rachel's gaze was enough to slice his gut, and he couldn't do a damned thing about it. There was no redeeming Matt or Matthew Shane.

That's why he needed to leave, to come to terms with who he was. He couldn't taint Tamela and his new child on a day-to-day basis with his old misdeeds. And good, honest men didn't have gambling debts. Not two hundred thousand dollars' worth.

Besides, it was obvious from the way Rachel had

glared at him after his revelation. She couldn't live with the old Matthew. And the fact that Matt was on the road to becoming his worst enemy meant she didn't want him around.

Matt absently pressed down on the accelerator. The trees were growing thicker on this stretch of road, casting such darkness that Matt could barely concentrate on the endless yellow dividing line. The sound of tires whirring over rainwater consumed him, luring him away from his disappointment.

God, he needed this blankness. He needed to clear his mind of everything except the road in front of him, a road laden with the smell of wet asphalt and leaves.

But jasmine layered the outdoor scent. So did thoughts of long, ash-brown hair and eyes the color of silvered water.

Rachel.

The name weighed heavily inside him, settling into his soul like a quilt covering a sleeping child.

But what else was sleeping within him? The urge to be with other women? The craving to enjoy a shot of whiskey slipping down his throat?

And what about the blonde and her boy? Where were they located in his mind, in his life?

Matt jerked the steering wheel to avoid a fallen tree branch, lying on the road like a corpse. He needed to slow down, to pay more attention.

He shook his head, as if that was going to loosen

a couple burdens. Yeah, right. He was a walking load of trouble.

He wasn't even sure where to go after the Edgewater Motel. How could he be a part of Tamela's and the baby's lives without running into Rachel? He couldn't avoid her, especially since she'd become so integral to him.

Integral?

The thought hit him like a slash of knife-edged pain.

She *was* his life.

So why the hell was he driving away from her?

He remembered the tears running down her cheeks as he'd left her standing in the doorway, remembered the "I love you."

He hadn't wanted to admit it, but he felt the same way.

Matt waited for the warning bells to go off inside his head, waited for instinct to scream at him for assuming the wrong thing.

But the emotion was true, growing with every passing second.

He loved her, and it scared the hell out of him.

So why was he driving in the opposite direction?

Jeez, he was an idiot. He needed to get his butt back to the farm, back to his family. His gut feeling had told him that all along. That's the reason he'd returned to Kane's Crossing in the first place.

He had to listen to his instinct, even if going back to Rachel would require more effort and patience.

But if he loved her, he'd stay.

Matt whipped the car around in a crazy U-turn, spraying rainwater as he skidded. Then he gunned the gas pedal, wanting to get home before Rachel had time to change her mind about loving him.

Funny how a difference in direction could make him feel better. All he could think about now was getting home and holding his family in his arms.

The rain had stopped, but the roads were still slick. Walls of water barricaded him on both sides, providing blinders.

That's the reason he didn't see the deer sprinting onto the road until it was too late.

He pumped the brakes, trying desperately to avoid the animal but, as he skidded closer, he knew it was unavoidable. Moments before the deer thudded into the car, Matt caught a flash of rounded brown eyes, then nothing.

As he stopped and threw open the door, he prayed that he hadn't killed the animal. He'd feel terrible. The creature lay on its side, blood seeping onto the road, the red matter mingling with the rain.

Matt kneeled, running his hands along its hide, seeking the injury. He found a gash along the deer's belly.

No heartbeat.

Matt's head sank, weighed down by guilt. As he dragged the body from the road, he could feel his own heart thrashing around his chest like a caged hawk.

He set the animal down, its head resting in Matt's

lap. He felt dizzy, his temples pounding. Most tellingly, his scar had started throbbing in time to his wild heartbeat.

Rain seeped into his jeans, as did the deer's blood. When Matt raised his palms, the car's headlights revealed that he was covered with the warm liquid; it ran down his arms, gathering under his nails.

His belly started shaking, the weakness traveling up to his blood-tinted hands. As the color red flowed over his sight, rage tore through his gut, tunneling its way to his brain.

Then the memories assaulted him.

His fear of failing as a father blanketed in a good, long swig of whiskey and joking friends he'd outgrown.

The phone call, the plea, the loan shark.

The image of a platinum blonde with her son.

Gumbo and Cajun music, blood splashed over the silver blade of a knife.

Blood on his clothing, on his hands.

Just like now.

The deer's blood seemed to have a life of its own, pulsing over Matt's skin. He looked down at the dead animal, then lay its head gently on the grass.

He couldn't think clearly. Couldn't concentrate. All Matt knew was that he'd killed an innocent animal.

He'd remembered a key moment from his past.

Oh, God, Matthew was back.

In a daze, he used his cell phone to call Sheriff

Reno, then followed the burble of a nearby running creek to its banks.

Blood. He had to get this blood off of him.

He kneeled by the flowing water, peering into its depths. It brought back the color of Rachel's eyes, especially when she cried. Cried because of Matthew.

Him.

The moon emerged for a full, fleeting moment, glimmering off the rocks. As Matt began to wash himself in the water, he saw grass waving in the current. The sight reminded him of this afternoon when he'd watched Rachel's hair sway with the rippling water. When he and Rachel had bathed each other, washing away the sweat of their lovemaking.

Matt closed his eyes, summoning images of the green-blue nightie and the woman who'd raked her nails down his back.

He wasn't afraid anymore.

Now he remembered how Rachel had worn that nightie one September night, standing in front of a window in their bedroom, the Kentucky wind fluttering the filmy material. Then they'd made love with such passion, she'd marked his back.

They'd laughed about it afterward, not knowing how the event would haunt him.

Relief flooded over Matt, but not entirely. He still had questions to go with the answers. He still wondered if he'd end up going back to his wild ways, wondered why his life had been spared if he wasn't good enough to deserve Rachel and their children.

Wondered what had happened to the blonde and her little boy now that he knew who they were.

Thank God, after Sam came and when Matt could finally go back home, he'd know the answers.

Matthew stood, ready to get on with his life as Matt, hoping Rachel would accept him when he knocked on her door.

Chapter Fifteen

Back at Green Oaks, Rachel hadn't been able to keep the sadness to herself.

She'd never been one to wail in grief to her friends. Sure, she'd joked about Matthew's disappearance, poking bitter reminders into dinner conversations and the like. But she'd never made a point of centering herself in a circle of comfort, warming herself in the spotlight of attention.

But she certainly had no shame tonight. She'd called Meg Cassidy who had, in turn, summoned the rest of the troops: her sister-in-law, Ashlyn Reno, plus Matt's sister, Lacey.

An all-star support system.

At the moment, they were in the family room, quietly consoling their friend while taking care not to disturb Tamela's sleep. Rachel hadn't possessed the strength to break the news of Matt's absence to their daughter. Not yet.

Meg placed a comforting hand on Rachel's. "He'll be back, honey. Men like Matt never really leave."

Lacey, who had shifted her carousel of fashion into a "Roaring Twenties chic" mode about a week ago, tucked a strand of bobbed hair behind her ear and spoke. "Since Rick lives near the Edgewater Motel, I put the guilt trip on him. He's cruising over there to hold some grunting sort of brother heart-to-heart with Matt."

Great, thought Rachel. In typical Kane's Crossing fashion, she'd managed to advertise her troubles to everyone.

But it felt good to be cared for.

Before she could thank them for the umpteenth time that night, a cry from Tamela's room ripped through the atmosphere.

Rachel bolted to her feet.

Another wail followed. "Mommy? Daddy?"

"Tam's having a bad dream," said Rachel. "I've got to go to her."

Meg asked, "What will you say?"

"What *should* I say?"

Silence. No one knew how to respond. Rachel supposed it was almost like talking to someone who'd just had a death in the family.

Ashlyn spoke first, nodding in the direction of her

son, Taggert, who was sleeping on a couch in the next room. "I can't imagine telling something like this to my own kid. Maybe she even heard Matt leave tonight."

Meg smiled at Rachel. "Go on upstairs. We can make you some tea, just like you did for me, when Nick was acting up."

Lacey twirled a strand of pearls around her neck. "Are men really worth all this grief?"

Ashlyn and Meg looked at each other. "Yes," they both said.

Rachel sighed and took a deep breath, then climbed the stairs, every slight creak a guilty reminder of how she'd goaded Matt to leave, how she should've appreciated him more.

Tamela sat stiffly in her bed when Rachel entered the room. The little girl's hair was wild with stray curls, tossed by her apparent dream.

She said, "Mommy, I dreamed that the whole town came into our house to spit on Daddy. And then I dreamed that Daddy jumped out a window and never came back."

Even the mention of Matt confused Rachel. A combination of sublime happiness, guilt and love weighed her down. What could she tell her daughter?

The girl rubbed her fists over her face. "Where's Daddy?"

She blinked and watched Rachel with serious brown eyes. Eyes that reflected Matt's. Rachel forced herself to look at the memento.

"Daddy had to go somewhere tonight."

Quick tears welled in Tamela's eyes. "Is it like before, when he was gone a long time?"

This was awful. Rachel's lower lip trembled as if she were a six-year-old kid herself. She didn't even know what to tell her daughter.

Tamela sat up straighter, bunching her pink comforter in her tiny fists. A tear spilled down her face. "Doesn't he love us?"

"Yes, he does. But it's complicated." Rachel cupped the girl's cheek, brushing a thumb over the wetness, wanting to wipe away the devastation, the red trail of abandonment. She could have been crying Tamela's hot tears, too, but it was her fault for letting Matt go.

She'd known damn well that he wasn't the same man he was before and, still, she'd thrown hateful accusations at him.

"Tam, honey," she said, "your father's a good man, and he deserves all of your love. Let's make that clear."

The girl stared at her mother, her jaw protruding in a juvenile show of defiance.

"Hey." Rachel softly held Tamela's chin between her thumb and forefinger. "I mean it. We're lucky to have him in our lives. If you're going to be angry with someone, be angry at me. It's taken a lot of time for your mom to get used to having Daddy back in our lives."

"Why?"

God, there was so much to say, so much Tamela wouldn't understand just yet. Frustration took over, scratching Rachel's throat with sadness. Wet heat filled her eyes, running down her cheeks.

Instead of words, her answer came out in a long-held sob. Rachel buried her face in her hands.

She'd been given another chance to repair her marriage, and what had she done? She'd thrown it away with her insecurities, with her inability to forgive.

And now she had to make it up to Tamela *and* the new baby.

Rachel felt a pair of small, soft hands encircling her wrists.

''Mommy?''

The hands pried Rachel's fingers away from her eyes. She saw Tamela's panicked face in front of her. ''Oh, baby, I'm so sorry,'' she said.

She held Tamela closely, her belly brushing against her daughter. As the little girl lay her head on Rachel's shoulder, Rachel felt Matt in Tamela's tears, felt him in the very slight curve of her stomach.

Months from now she'd be round with his second child. The thought consoled her, floated a veil of serenity over her.

Her friends had been right. Telling Tamela the truth had felt good. Rachel should have practiced honesty years ago, to her father regarding her mother's affairs, to herself during the hard years of her marriage.

Fighting an invisible enemy as powerful as lies was

next to impossible. Truth would've helped her, healed her.

Truth would've stabilized her marriage to Matthew. She wondered if her husband would ever find the whole truth about himself.

She wished she could've helped him.

Time passed in a blur as they lay in bed, Tamela falling asleep in Rachel's arms. She'd cuddled against her mother's belly, as if sensing the new addition to the family.

Rachel hadn't told her about the baby yet, but she would come morning.

The next thing she knew, someone was whispering in her ear, waking her from a peaceful stretch of sleep.

Lacey's silhouette stood before the rain-splattered window. Without a word, Rachel stood and hugged her sister-in-law.

Lacey whispered, "I know. I've missed my brother, too."

They embraced again, then Lacey bent to lift Tamela in her arms. "You need to go downstairs," she said softly. "Meg's going to take Tamela home with her tonight."

A mixture of fear and anticipation jabbed Rachel in the heart. "Is Matt back?"

Lacey nodded. "He never made it to the motel, I guess, so don't be surprised if Rick shows up to check on him. You might want to hash things out while you have privacy."

She didn't know if she could stand seeing him again. Didn't know if she couldn't stand it, either.

As Lacey took the slumbering Tamela with her, Rachel stayed in the dark of her daughter's bedroom, listening to her heart pound, still wondering why Matt had returned.

Was she ready for Matthew? Or would it still be Matt?

She walked down the stairs, her trepidation echoing through every beat of blood pumping through her body.

Once she'd reached the foyer, Rachel noticed that Meg, Lacey and Ashlyn had already left. Her home fairly pulsed with emptiness.

That's when she noticed that the front door was cracked open. A slit of cold air breathed through the space, beckoning her.

With a deep breath, she stepped forward and opened the door.

Matt stood in the center of the porch's light, hat off, his body rain steeped. His dark hair flopped in a damp slouch over his forehead, and his denim shirt and jeans molded every muscle of his body. As he unfolded his arms, he assumed a wary stance, hands bunched at his sides. Even his burnt-scar gaze reflected his doubt, casting the charred slant of a frown over his lips.

For a second, time suspended itself, poised in mid-air as if it were a leaping animal caught by a bullet.

Rachel's emotions gathered, exploding on the edge of a sob as she threw herself into his arms.

Matt caught his wife, wrapping his arms around her warm body. She smelled of sleep and jasmine muskiness, and he tightened his grip.

She spoke into his chest. "I don't care what happened before, Matt. I don't even care what you did with that money."

He knew that she was speaking from emotion, probably feeling as grateful as he did to be holding each other again. "I remember my life, Rachel."

Matt braced himself for her reaction, but all she did was raise her head, look him in the eye and pull him down for a long, welcome-home kiss.

It was what he'd been hoping for that first day back.

He breathed her in, feeling comfortable with the scent of her shampoo, her soap, her warmth.

He'd hoped for this sense of security back in New Orleans, back on the Texas ranch where he'd worked under a name he'd picked from the air.

Matt was home again.

When she pulled away from his lips, she sketched her thumb over them. "I want you the way you are now."

A flare of desire quickened his blood. "Before you go making any promises, I've got a lot to tell you."

She waited, her gray-green gaze showing understanding, compassion. And an encouraging warmth.

He led her to the stone steps, where they both sat, Rachel linking an arm through his, resting her hand on his thigh. He palmed the top of that hand.

"You'll hear the Kane's Crossing grapevine quaking with the news tomorrow," he said. "A deer crashed into the car tonight. I held its head while blood coated my hands, while it died. And I saw my life through Matthew's eyes. I saw what happened."

He didn't bother to tell her that Deputy Gary Joanson had alerted the Kentucky Department of Fish and Wildlife to pick up the carcass, and that a surprisingly supportive Sam Reno had dropped Matt back at his own doorstep.

Rachel had rested her other hand on his bicep, her grip firm as a buttress. "What happened?" she asked.

The memories crashed over him. "I'd gotten a call at the office from a fraternity brother. Remember Norman Wolper?"

She nodded, and Matt continued, his college friend's cherubic, pink-flushed face flooding his mind.

"Norman was down in New Orleans. He apologized, said he wouldn't have called if it hadn't been such an emergency, but loan sharks were on his tail. Norman had done a little too much gambling, and he was in big trouble."

Hope glowed in Rachel's eyes. She'd probably figured out that it hadn't been Matt's gambling problem that sucked up their two hundred thousand dollars. "But Norman was a good kid in college," she said.

"In front of females," said Matt. Cupid-sweet Norman would open doors for his dates, then make silly, crude gestures behind them. "The guy always had a wild streak. But he was fun, witty, always the life of the party."

Just as Matthew had been. But never to the extent of Norman. "Norman was just out of control. He'd gotten himself into a situation where he needed cash right away.

"Two hundred and fifty thousand dollars, all in thousand-dollar bills. I might've thought twice about the request if he hadn't told me that the loan shark had threatened to harm Norman's wife and child unless he paid off the money."

And that's where the platinum blonde and the boy had come into the picture. Norman had kept a picture of his family with him to the very end, even when it had been washed over with his blood.

When Matt had made the connection, relief had almost swallowed him whole. He'd never had a second family; he'd merely protected someone else's.

He glanced at Rachel to gauge her reaction. She was watching him with a new understanding, a new tilt to her head, a sheen of tears in her eyes. "I wish I'd known that you were playing the benevolent hero, Matt."

"Me, too." One part of him couldn't believe she was accepting his explanation without a jaded angle to her brow. Was she finally willing to trust him?

God, he hoped so.

"There's more," he said. "I thought I could take

care of this situation quickly, and there wasn't enough time to explain Norman's predicament to you. So I withdrew the money from the bank, thinking I could deal with it later, and hoping the amount would be enough to keep the loan shark satisfied until Norman could come up with the rest of the money. Then I flew down to New Orleans that day. I wanted to go there myself with the cash, especially since Norman's greed and irresponsibility had gotten him into this fix in the first place. I needed to know his family would be safe."

Rachel peered at the wet grass below them. A smattering of raindrops had fallen from the skies, dotting her bare feet with a misty cover. "At that point in our marriage, I don't know if I would've been easy to approach. We didn't talk very much back then. Lots of times we'd just communicate through your administrative assistant."

Matt pressed a kiss to her forehead. "I guess it wasn't unheard of for me to take short business trips and then return to Louisville for the night."

Rachel nodded, leaning into him. "Right. There were times you didn't even come home. Rick would fly you to Louisville in his plane, and you'd just stay there for days in a hotel."

"And that's why you thought I was having an affair." Hell, he'd been thinking the same thing himself. How could he blame her? "Rachel, I never broke our marriage vows. Can you tell me that you believe me?"

She lifted her head, locking gazes with him. Softly she said, "My heart's telling me to believe you. And I do."

He grinned. "Thank the good Lord."

Then he blew out a breath, drawing a wistful smile from his wife.

"Anyway," he continued, "I thought I'd hop a quick flight to the Big Easy, help out Norman then do a little Bourbon Street sightseeing and be back in Louisville the next day." Matt paused. "I liked my drink. Liked shirking my responsibility to you and Tamela by hanging out with Sonny and Junior at the pool hall."

Tamela's family Crayola picture surfaced in his mind's eye. Suddenly, he understood the reason he'd been so out of breath, so disturbed by the drawing.

"I was afraid of committing to the both of you, Rache. When you got pregnant, I lost it. I thought, 'Hey, that's the end of my youth.' I didn't want to let go of that. Dammit, I know I was a selfish jerk, but I really didn't know how to handle a family. I just wasn't ready."

"I thought you didn't love me anymore."

"No," he said, stroking her cheek with a finger. "I was an idiot. A Peter Pan."

"We've wasted a lot of time." She pressed her cheek into his arm.

The sprinkle of rain had swelled into fatter droplets, but neither of them moved. To do so might break this spell of honesty, and Matt couldn't risk it.

So he pulled her closer, sheltering her with his body, wondering if he'd also been struck by fear at the sight of Tamela's picture because it had reminded him of Norman's own family and the danger they'd escaped.

The mere thought of it spiked his heartbeat. "I met Norman in a dingy restaurant on the fringes of the city. We had gumbo for dinner, listened to some Cajun music. Then we watched women with too much makeup and black skirts up to their armpits as they leaned over the chairs, showing us their cleavage and inviting us on dates. It was just like college."

"Prostitutes," said Rachel, a measure of jealousy in her voice.

"I didn't look twice," said Matt, running a finger down the slope of her nose. "Besides, we had business to take care of. It put a damper on the festivities, to say the least. Norman even looked a little pale. He was scared about the missing fifty thousand. He must've known the shark would go ballistic."

Rachel asked, "How could he have been so stupid?"

"Norman was a drunk. Receding hairline, bloated stomach, the works. I remember thinking, 'Is this what I'm going to look like in a year?' He scared me to death, Rache, and he disgusted me. *I* disgusted me. So I put aside the alcohol that night."

The expression on Rachel's face said it all: *Would you have stayed sober when you got home?*

Matt couldn't vouch much for his intentions, but

he really had ended up living the clean life. His amnesia had spanked all cravings for booze right out of him.

"I'd already agreed to be with Norman during the payoff," he said. "I thought, 'Big deal, right? We'll just give the guy his money, promise to come up with some more and we're off the hook.' But that's not how it went."

A shot of pain ripped through his temples, but Matt fought it off. Instead, the fear of the next events materialized in his hammering heartbeat, his difficulty in breathing.

"We met the shark and his henchmen on a quiet street, behind a bar. It was deserted, and I knew in my gut that it wasn't the smart thing to do, but Norman insisted it was okay. He'd dealt with this guy before. Louis the Frenchman, they called him, like he was some dapper gentleman. We should've expected his anger. He wanted all his money, and Norman just didn't have it."

Matt took a moment to steady his emotions, his body. Facing this part of the memory sapped his strength. As he hesitated, rain dripped down his hair, over his shoulders, a sorry comfort against the throb of his scar.

It had rained that night, too. "When we told Louis that we didn't have the requested amount, he went crazy, summoned his thugs. Those guys flashed their knives in our faces. I suppose they didn't want to draw attention with gunshots. I took out my wallet, but I didn't have much. One of the guys howled with laughter and slapped the wallet out of my hands. And then, before I knew what was happening, one of those thugs knifed Norman in the gut and grabbed the money. Then I was belted over the head with a board.''

Rachel ran her fingers through his hair, mapping his injuries. Her touch eased his pain like a sedative.

The next few images all ran together, separated by splinters of a second. ''Then I just remember feeling the knife cut my skin, but I was too nauseous to care. Norman fell against me, and then there was blood on my shirt. I knew he was dead. And that's when everything goes black in my mind, with just this little pinprick of color.''

Rachel said, ''Maybe your brain was protecting you from the trauma by blocking it out.''

''I needed all the help I could get. I think I did the only thing that would save my life. Someone yelled nearby, and I took the opportunity to run from the thugs. That's all I remember before it all went black. Next thing I knew, a wino was going through my already-empty pockets.''

Rachel kissed him again, murmuring, ''I'm so lucky to have you alive.''

Matt nodded. Still, why had he been the one to survive? Why had fate chosen to take Norman instead of Matthew?

He turned to her. ''I haven't lived a perfect life—

you know that firsthand. Are you going to be able to forgive me for screwing up?''

Her hesitation held aeons of self-hatred for Matt. Why should she forgive him?

"I know," he said, gritting his teeth. "Why do I deserve to live when my friend died? I've been asking myself since I regained my memory. I've asked myself why I'm alive when I couldn't save Norman. What gives me the right to have a second chance?''

She cleared her throat. "Can I interrupt your brow-beating for a second? I forgive you. I just can't believe we have that second chance. It's almost like someone knew we had to start over again to make a go of our marriage.''

By this time, the rain was really sparkling, streaming from above with a cleansing energy. Even if their clothes were soaked, even if water was coursing down their faces like a thousand tears, Matt didn't care.

"You can forgive me for being an inattentive husband? For being a scared-out-of-his-gourd father?''

Rachel stood, keeping hold of his hand.

"Can you forgive *me* of my lack of trust? My inability to do *my* part in the marriage?''

He could only smile and nod.

She said, "Sometimes the mistakes we make can be powerful lessons. As long as you never forget—and I never forget—our shortcomings, I think we've got a shot.''

He followed her lead, standing, pulling her into his arms. "I should never have hidden behind my work,

Rache. I shouldn't have thought it was my right to extend youth to its limits. I almost ruined this marriage, and you can be damned sure it won't happen again.''

He slipped his hand down to her belly, imagining the life forming behind her skin. He'd helped to create this life.

His chest tightened. Too much emotion. Too much time lost.

Pressing his mouth to her ear, he said, ''I'm going to love you until I die. No matter who I am, or what I've done in the past.'' She sank against his body, but he held her up.

''Well,'' she said through the threat of sobs, ''you did a fine job of surviving the first time, so don't be talking about death, Matt.''

It seemed as if Rachel's smile chased away some of the rain, because it let up, dropping off to a hazy summer shower.

She said, ''If you're still wondering why you were kept alive, it's because you needed to come back to me and your child. It's because we were meant to have another one, too. We need you. We love you.''

As if her statement required proof, she slipped the wedding ring from her finger.

Rain misted over them, washing them into the next step of their lives.

She said, ''I wore this the whole time you were gone. To me, I was always married to the man I'd first fallen in love with. Nothing was going to change that.''

The ring, plus a flood of relief, warmed his skin as she eased it over his pinkie. The entwined roses and thorns caught his eye, reminding him of the beauties and beasts of marriage.

She'd never loved another man.

She smiled up at him. ''Every time you look at that ring, I want you to think of my love and how it's going to last forever. No matter what happens.''

He touched it, liking the comfort of its fit. ''I don't have a ring to give to you right now.''

''Don't worry. You never wore one.'' She rubbed a palm over his chest, over his heart. ''Besides, you've already given me back my life, Matt. Nothing can compare to that.''

He grasped her fingers, traced the tan line her ring had stamped on her skin. The imprint of her other hand was leaving a heated mark on his skin, shooting desire through his veins.

''I love you,'' he said, lowering his mouth to hers.

She held her fingers against his lips. ''You promise to keep your appointments with those big-city doctors? I want that head looked after.''

He slanted her a grin. ''Yes, ma'm. And you'll discontinue the services of Chloe Lister?''

''Of course.''

As he bent his head again, she pressed her fingers more firmly to him. ''And no more secrets. Right?''

He grabbed her hand and planted a slow kiss on it. She shivered under his touch.

"No more secrets. Ever."

She smiled and leaned up for his kiss. When their lips connected, he no longer felt the rain on his skin. He was only aware of her body molded against his, of his child growing within that body.

They might have stayed outside for hours, just tasting and caressing each other like young kids—like they used to do when they'd first started dating. But the rain started to fall again, pelting them with tiny fists.

He raised his head, keeping her tightly ensconced in his arms. "I vote we go inside."

"I second that."

They held hands as they walked up the steps and into the light and dry solitude of the porch.

As Rachel opened the door to let him back in, Matt's instinct screamed to look behind him.

Beneath a nearby elm tree, shaded by the branches, stood a dark figure, the glow of a cigar flaring in the rain-swept black of night. His face was hidden from the glare of the porch light, but Matt knew who it was.

Even though his younger brother didn't like him, he'd come to see to his safety.

Rachel tugged on his hand, and Matt turned to her, thinking he'd solve his family problems another day. His wife was so beautiful, her dress a tight layer of sheer nothingness against her swollen breasts and long legs, her mouth red from his kisses, her eyes a glowing invitation for him to come home.

Matt glanced once more at Rick and nodded. The rounded-burn of cigar ash bobbed in return, disappearing as the wounded shadow turned back the way it had come.

Matt faced Rachel and, as she led him into her life once again, he felt the heat of his scar melt back into him.

Filling the empty space just below his heart.

Epilogue

The following April brought a postwinter crisp to Kane's Crossing, but that didn't bother the family in front of the fireplace at Green Oaks.

As Matt held baby Dawn, swathed in her nursery blanket on his lap, they were both warmed to an orange glow by the fire's flames. He was in the process of dabbing some fussy tears from the two-month-old's squinty eyes.

Rachel's heart swelled with happiness. Dawn had been an easy pregnancy, not only physically but because Matt, the epitome of a worried dad, had been with them minute by minute.

He'd been that way with Dolly Llama, too, when she'd foaled. Rachel and Matt were already fielding queries from prospective buyers, and the foal would no doubt be selling for a healthy sum at a private yearling sale, fetching enough money to keep the horse farm afloat and out of Tarkin's grasp.

Tamela bounded up from her seat, a crayon-colored picture in her hands. "See, Daddy? Am I a good drawer?"

Matt peered over Dawn's fuzzy head to peruse the piece of art. For a minute, Rachel remembered how he'd reacted to the family picture last summer, before all his hospital tests had cleared him of further injuries.

But she shouldn't have worried about any of it. He smiled at Tamela, then at Rachel, adding a wink. "Call Peter Tarkin, Mom. He might want to add this to his collection."

Tamela sprinted over to Rachel, bearing her drawing. "Look? See?"

The image boasted a family of four, with the little girl—whom Rachel assumed to be her curly-headed elder daughter—brandishing a sword.

"That is exceptional, Tam."

The little girl flashed a smile and went back to the drawing board.

Rachel took a seat on the carpet by her husband, lifting her face to the fire's heat. "My dad called this morning."

Matt leaned in, resting his lips under her jawline. His voice was muffled when he asked, "And?"

"And…" She played with the ring on her finger—

the one created from melting down the Spanish original to make one ring for her, and one for Matt. "He suspects Mom of having an affair. I've got to visit them, to work this out. I'm not going to lie or make excuses for her anymore."

Her husband gazed at her, his smile rounding like the curve of a heart. "You're strong enough for the both of them, Rache."

Matt himself had taken an important trip before they'd had Dawn. He'd visited Norman's wife and son, making sure they were healthy and safe in the wake of Norman's death. Even now, they corresponded with Matt, just to say they were doing all right.

Of course, Matt had never told them the sordid details. There were some subjects best left unsaid. But he had told Mrs. Wolper why Norman had died.

A husband who took care of his responsibilities. That was her Matt Shane, through and through.

Dawn shone a gummy smile at her father as Matt dried the remainder of her tears.

"She trusts you so much," said Rachel. "She'd even let you balance her on your fingertip."

The wind blew a soulful tune around their home, tapping branches against the windows, reminding her of the outside forces that affected a marriage: a stranger coming in from the heat of a summer to reclaim his home. A lack of trust wedging a couple apart.

Distrust had been the stranger in their marriage, and Rachel was thankful for the day it had disappeared.

She leaned in to her husband's muscle-bunched arm, snuggling her lips against his ear. "I'd trust you to balance me on a fingertip any day."

His half smile sent a zing to places she'd only dreamt existed. "We need to test that idea, Rache."

As their lips pressed together in a heart-flipping kiss, Rachel knew one thing for certain.

There would be no more strangers in her house. Not as long as love stayed home.

* * * * *

SILHOUETTE
SPECIAL EDITION

AVAILABLE FROM 21ST NOVEMBER 2003

RYAN'S PLACE Sherryl Woods

The Devaneys

Ryan Devaney didn't believe in love—until he met Maggie O'Brien. Her bright smile and tender touch warmed his frozen spirit and awakened forgotten desires—but dare Ryan dream of a happily-ever-after?

SCROOGE AND THE SINGLE GIRL
Christine Rimmer

The Sons of Caitlin Bravo

All Will Bravo wanted for the festive season was to be left alone. Then in walked beautiful Jilly Diamond, who tempted him beyond all reason. Suddenly Jilly was *everything* Will desired for Christmas.

THEIR INSTANT BABY Cathy Gillen Thacker

The Deveraux Legacy

When Amy Deveraux agreed to babysit her godson she hadn't known she'd be sharing her duties with sexy Nick Everton. But seeing Nick with the baby made Amy yearn for something *much* more permanent.

THE COWBOY'S CHRISTMAS MIRACLE
Anne McAllister

Code of the West

Single mum Erin Jones had never expected to see her unrequited crush Deke Malone again—especially not with a two-year-old son! His maleness set Erin on fire—but would they get a second chance at love?

RACE TO THE ALTAR Patricia Hagan

Under different circumstances racing driver Rick Castles would've stopped at nothing to make Liz Mallory his. But his career hurt relationships. *Could* he risk the ultimate race with Liz—to the altar?

HER SECRET AFFAIR Arlene James

A business contract was all Chey and millionaire Brodie Todd were supposed to have. Except they couldn't stop their overwhelming attraction. But could Chey risk her heart on this powerful, handsome single father?

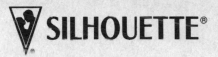

Celebrate the joys of Christmas
with three wonderful romances
from favourite Silhouette authors

Midnight Clear

Debbie Macomber

Lindsay McKenna

Stella Bagwell

On sale 21st November 2003

He is every inch a Desperado.
But this time the job is personal.

Diana
Palmer

DESPERADO

FREE!

4 Books
and a surprise gift!

We would like to take this opportunity to thank you for reading this Silhouette® book by offering you the chance to take FOUR more specially selected titles from the Special Edition™ series absolutely FREE! We're also making this offer to introduce you to the benefits of the Reader Service™ —

- ★ FREE home delivery
- ★ FREE gifts and competitions
- ★ FREE monthly Newsletter
- ★ Books available before they're in the shops
- ★ Exclusive Reader Service discount

Accepting these FREE books and gift places you under no obligation to buy; you may cancel at any time, even after receiving your free shipment. Simply complete your details below and return the entire page to the address below. *You don't even need a stamp!*

YES! Please send me 4 free Special Edition books and a surprise gift. I understand that unless you hear from me, I will receive 6 superb new titles every month for just £2.90 each, postage and packing free. I am under no obligation to purchase any books and may cancel my subscription at any time. The free books and gift will be mine to keep in any case.

E3ZEF

Ms/Mrs/Miss/Mr ....Initials...............................
BLOCK CAPITALS PLEASE

Surname...

Address...

....

....Postcode ....

Send this whole page to:
UK: The Reader Service, FREEPOST CN81, Croydon, CR9 3WZ
EIRE: The Reader Service, PO Box 4546, Kilcock, County Kildare (stamp required)